Books by Mark Lee Taylor

A PEBBLE TOSSED

FOUL TERRITORY

MANAIA (part of the anthology FORGOTTEN, edited by Keith J. Hoskins)

Murder at Double Groove

Mark Lee Taylor

This book is a work of fiction. Double Groove Brewing Company® and Not Just Vacs are actual businesses in Forest Hill, Maryland. Their names and descriptions are used with permission of the owners. All Double Groove staff members in this book are actual people whose names and descriptions have also been used with permission. Some artistic liberties have been taken, but for the most part these people are as represented, and the author hopes you get to meet them. The same applies to Bobby Buckley and his sons Evan and Kyle, Regis and Angela Burke, Mike and Michele DiPietro, John and Sue Harris, Phyllis Hemmes, Mike Karavas, Rick and Stella Rineer, Mike Strazzire, Carmella Taylor, and Amy Willig, all of whom are actual Double Groove regulars who kindly gave permission for their names and descriptions to be used fictitiously in this book. It also applies to Craig and Donna Willig, former part-owners of Double Groove, and Jim and Lori Geckle, the cover artist and his wife, who also kindly granted permission to use their names. The Willig Boys, Radio Religion, Second Wind, and The Russ and Johnny Show are actual musical performing acts who kindly gave permission for their names and descriptions to be used fictitiously in this book. Marlin (like the fish) is based on the author's father, brought back to life herein by the magic of fiction.

All other names, characters, businesses, and organizations are either products of the author's imagination or used fictitiously. Aside from those listed above, any resemblance to actual persons living or dead is entirely coincidental.

As of this writing, no actual murders have ever occurred at Double Groove Brewing. No actual animals were kicked or otherwise harmed in the writing of this novel. Your mileage may vary.

Lyrics to "Hangin' Out at Double Groove," by Jeffrey John Willig, used by kind permission of the songwriter.

Copyright © 2024 by Mark Lee Taylor

Cover art Copyright © 2024 by James P. Geckle

All rights reserved, including the right to reproduce this book or any portion thereof in any form whatsoever.

ISBN: 9798334762565
ASIN: B0DCNJYQ7Z

DEDICATION

This book is lovingly dedicated to the memory of Marlin Taylor (1936-2022), whose name, likeness, and mannerisms I callously ripped off without his permission. I'm sure he wouldn't mind.

I miss you every day, Pop.

Now, listen at me ...

—Marlin Taylor

CHAPTER ONE

THE PERFECT TIME to kill your husband never seemed to arrive. *But today,* Christine Buckley thought, *is about as close as it gets.* She raked spent grain out of the mash tun, wincing in pain as she tried to put as little weight on her left ankle as possible.

"You want me to take over there?" Mark, her boss, asked. "You look like you're struggling." Mark, while not a bruiser by any stretch, was accustomed to the work. It may have even been why he, at fifty-something, still possessed the body and musculature of a man ten to fifteen years younger.

"I'm good," Christine said, pushing her glasses up her nose, which had grown slick with sweat. "Tripped over one of my husband's boots this morning and sprained my ankle. It's a little sore, but I'll manage."

Mark smiled as he turned to write a series of dates on the whiteboard. "The boot's fault, I guess."

"Nope," she said with a grin of her own. "The husband's fault. He left it right in front of the door."

Mark Moody, co-owner and head brewmaster of Double Groove Brewing, snickered. "Are you sure it was Bobby's and not yours?"

Christine, employed at Double Groove as a brewer and bartender, was silent for a breath or two before she replied. "Pretty much."

"Pretty much?"

"Well, I was in a hurry, and I didn't have time to look behind me. But it was big. Big enough to trip over."

"I get that."

"It *had* to have been his."

"That settles it then," Mark said.

Christine shot a glance at Mark, but he was facing the whiteboard, so she couldn't read his expression. "Are you humoring me right now? Because I'm thinking about killing him when I get home."

"As is fitting," he said as he turned to face her. "But we have that book release party tonight. I want to transfer this "Gimme Three Hops" into the brite beer tank so we can get it canned tomorrow, and then I want to clean the brewhouse up so it'll be ready for anybody that wants to tour it later. Think you can put off killing Bobby long enough to help me out?"

"Sure," she said with a smile. "I wouldn't miss this party anyway." She knew, and knew that Mark knew, that there would be no killing of husbands tonight, or ever. At least as far as the two of them and their respective spouses, whom they each loved dearly.

As Mark began the process of transferring the wort from the boil kettle to one of the fermentation tanks, Christine scraped the last of the wet grain out of the 155-gallon mash tun, and into five-gallon buckets, which would later be picked up by a local farm, to be used as feed for their livestock. Then she hosed out the mash tun and rinsed the floor, watching the water and bits of grain disappear into the trench drain that ran the length of the room.

Double Groove was a small craft brewery nestled in the rolling hills and tall maples of Forest Hill, Maryland. They kept a rotating selection of fourteen beers on tap at all times, the signature brew of which was an India Pale Ale known as "Gimme Three Hops," a pun based on a popular Lynyrd Skynyrd song. All their brews had similar names based on classic rock songs.

Mark and Christine stood in the production area of the brewery, sometimes referred to as the brewhouse. Dominated on brew days like today by the pervasive grainy odor of boiling wort, this was where the magic happened. It was a huge, two-story room, dominated by rows of stainless steel vats taller than most humans, along with assorted pipes, conduits, refrigerant lines, gauges, lights, and buzzers, not to mention bells and whistles. To the uninitiated, the whole experience was dizzying. To Christine, Mark, and the rest of the staff, it was home.

"I do need to go home and change clothes before the party, though," Christine said. Her bib overalls and rubber boots would never do if she was to meet Janis O'Riordan in person. On top of that, she smelled like a ghastly commingling of wort and sweat after working all morning in the non-climate-controlled brewhouse.

"I'm sure we can make that happen," Mark said. "Here, think fast."

Christine turned just in time to catch the old tennis ball Mark had tossed her way.

"Damn, Mark," she said with the grungy, smelly orb clutched in her fist. "A little more warning?"

Mark doubled over in laughter. "If you could've seen your face."

"Very funny." A four-inch-high soapstone wall ran across the brewhouse to separate the wet half from the dry half, and Christine dropped the ball behind this ledge and kept shoveling, thinking she'd whip the ball back at Mark when he least suspected. "Why is there a tennis ball in here, anyway?"

"Somebody left it in the taproom yesterday." *Somebody* meaning a dog. Mark and his wife Lisa were devoted dog lovers, and Double Groove catered to others like them. All dogs, unless they were overly aggressive, were welcome in the taproom.

Most evenings, a cast of small-town regulars would filter into the taproom one by one or in pairs, take seats at the bar, choose albums to play from the voluminous collection of vinyl kept behind the bar, drink the county's best beer, and chew the fat as might be done in millions of local corner pubs across the country. Double Groove had been conceived by Mark, Lisa, and former part-owners Craig and Donna as a local neighborhood bar in the vein of Cheers, and it had achieved that goal in spades.

But tonight, the regulars would be overwhelmed by a gathering of Janis O'Riordan fans.

Ms. O'Riordan was the closest thing the suburban county had to a local celebrity, and perhaps not coincidentally, was related to one of Double Groove's bartenders. While not exactly a *New York Times* Bestselling Author, she was revered in the somewhat insular world of cozy mystery writers. Christine herself was an ardent follower of the author's *Gunpowder River Mysteries* and was eager to meet her. And maybe get a book signed. Or two. Or five.

She stole a glance in Mark's direction. There he stood with his back to her, studying one of the ferm tanks over the top of his readers. Christine was tall and had long arms, and she knew how to throw out a runner at first. "Hey," she said, and she whipped the tennis ball into his back, where it struck with an audible smack and fell to the floor.

Mark turned and gave her a hurt look.

"I tried to warn you," she said with a shrug.

"Sheesh," he said, rubbing his back. "Where'd you get that arm, from throwing axes?"

Christine laughed. The question was an oblique reference to her nickname, "Viking," bestowed upon her by the staff because of her height and her long blond hair.

She turned as she heard the door between the brewhouse and the taproom open, and bartender Megan Gravell entered. Megan had obviously seen the throw through the glass door, and held out her hands for the ball, grinning. "Are we throwing stuff at Mark today? My turn."

Mark chuckled. "I think maybe—"

"Wait, I got a better idea," Megan said as she grabbed a one-inch diameter transfer pipe off its hanger on the wall. She took her stance and waved the four-foot length of stainless steel like a batter at the plate. "Give me your best pitch."

"I think we need to settle down before we snap a fitting off, or this nasty old thing ends up in the mash tun," Mark said as he dropped the ball in a five-gallon bucket.

"Party pooper," Megan said as she hung the pipe back on the wall where she'd found it. "You're scared of me; I get it. Everybody is, that's why Purple Crush keeps winning." Megan had been an avid softball player since high school, and ten or fifteen years down the road, she still played, and she still had a slugger's muscular physique. "Anyway, I just came in to tell you that the Rye of the Tiger keg ran dry."

"Already?" Mark said. "What time is it?"

"Twelve-oh-five, honey," Megan said, smiling sweetly.

"And who ordered the Rye of the Tiger five minutes after opening time, as if I didn't know?"

"The sheriff."

"Knew it! Okay, I'll get right on it."

Mark followed Megan back through the door and disappeared into the cold room on the left to change the keg.

Christine finished shoveling and picked up a mop to start cleaning up leftover liquid from the wet grain. Mark came back into the brewhouse, and together, over the next hour, they finished cleaning up. Then Mark held the door for her as they both went into the taproom, dragging behind them the yeasty smell of beer being born, and joined Megan behind the bar.

Uriah Heep's *Demons and Wizards* filled the room at a volume loud enough to appreciate, but low enough to talk over. At Double Groove, the motto was *Taste, Chill, Listen*, and unless there was a live band, they played vinyl albums in the taproom all day. Classic rock album covers completely covered one entire wall, and a painted mural of a stereo system occupied the opposite one. Any leftover wall space was peppered with concert posters, guitars, and beer posters, even in all four unisex bathrooms. The name Double Groove itself was based on a feature found on some rare vinyl records, wherein each side of the disc was inscribed with two separate and distinct grooves, so that a different set of songs played depending on where on the circumference of the record the needle was set down.

It was almost two o'clock on a Saturday, and several patrons were seated at the bar. Most of the tables were still empty, but Phyllis Hemmes, a retired Phys Ed teacher, sat alone at a corner table shuffling papers and drinking beer, and a man and woman Christine didn't know sat at a table on the opposite side of the taproom, quietly talking to each other and drinking Irish Red Skies, a beer that could be identified at a glance by its color.

Mark slid behind Megan to talk to Sheriff Alan Curtis,

who sat at the end of the B-Side bar. Beside the sheriff sat Deputy Ronnie Gaines, a younger man with tightly trimmed black hair who caught Christine's eye and smiled. Both men were out of uniform, as was appropriate, considering that they were consuming alcohol at a brewpub.

"Hey, Alan," Mark said. "I heard you blew out my Rye of the Tiger again."

Alan laughed. "I consider it my sacred duty."

"Well done," Mark said, "well d—" Mark fell silent as he noticed the couple by the window. His face darkened. "Could you excuse me a second?"

He passed from behind the bar and approached the table as the couple turned to face him. At first, Christine couldn't hear what was being said, but she could tell by Mark's face that he wasn't happy, and by the other man's gesticulations that he wasn't either.

Uh-oh. Mark could be a sweetheart and the best of friends, but it was never a good idea to get under his skin. Christine silently wished for the other guy to back down, whatever their dispute was.

Nope. Things ramped up, and voices got louder. "It was for a year," the man said. "The year's up, as of yesterday."

"Fine," Mark said. "You're banned again. Get out."

"You can't do that!" the man said, his long reddish beard waggling in time with his chin.

"I can, and I just did."

Ronnie Gaines turned to see what the ruckus was about and got off his stool, setting his beer on the bar.

Alan Curtis smiled and lifted his beer for a sip.

Mark, catching Ronnie out of the corner of his eye, held up his palm to stay him. "Just get out," he repeated to the patron. "You're not welcome here."

"Can I finish my beer?" the man's companion asked.

"You can stay if you want. He's gotta go. Now."

The couple got up from their chairs. The woman deliberately knocked her glass over, and Irish Red Skies gushed across the table and onto the floor. The man cast a bloodshot glare at Mark as he shoved the door open hard enough to cause it to bang against the outside wall, and he exited the taproom. The woman flipped the bird at Mark as she left in his wake.

The door drifted closed, and "Rainbow Demons" on the speakers became the only sound in the room. All conversation had stopped.

"What was that all about?" Megan asked for everybody.

"Since this place opened, I've only had to throw three people out of here," Mark said. "That was one of them. His name is Keith Bonham."

"What'd he do?" Megan asked.

"Year ago yesterday, he got obnoxious and … I don't wanna say belligerent, but kind of pushy, I guess you could say. Bumping into people and making a nuisance of himself. On a beer and a half, which I found kind of weird. And in the bathroom I found two empty vodka miniatures in the trash can."

"The same day?"

"Yup."

"That'd explain it," Alan said.

Mark nodded. "*If* they were his. I wasn't positive at the time. I mean, maybe he just had a low tolerance for alcohol, you know? But when I saw him come out of the bathroom again, I went right in behind him and I found *another* mini."

"Oops," Christine said. "Gotcha."

"That's a no-no," said Megan, waggling her forefinger. By law, no outside alcohol was allowed in Double Groove.

"I explained that to him, and he got in my face. So I banned him for a year."

"And the year ended yesterday," Alan said.

"Yeah. And he figured he could come back today, but I just informed him otherwise."

"Fill out the Banning Letter," Alan said, "and I'll sign it right now."

Misbehavior was uncommon at Double Groove. In the first place, it was rare to come across combative drunks in *any* brewpub. The beer was expensive, and the people who drank it did so because they appreciated the taste and the artisanship that went into its making, not to get drunk and start fights. On top of that, it was well known that Double Groove often had a few off-duty cops in attendance.

"I had your back," Ronnie said.

"I know you did, and I appreciate it," Mark said. "But I want this to be a place where you guys don't need to bring your work."

Ronnie nodded and sat back down.

Alan, who through it all hadn't diverted his attention from his beer, said, "I never doubted you, Mark." There was general laughter around the bar.

But Christine looked out the front picture window and saw that Keith Bonham was still outside, sitting at a picnic table at the edge of the premises, apparently arguing with his wife or girlfriend or whatever she was to him.

And she wondered if this was really over.

CHAPTER TWO

CHRISTINE DID, IN fact, get a chance to make a quick trip home and freshen up. Before leaving the Groove, she noticed that Keith Bonham and his lady friend had disappeared. That was good. She didn't need any worries like that polluting her day.

On the way home, she daydreamed, and when she daydreamed, of course she daydreamed about '41 Ford Pickups.

She *wanted* one. With a deep passion.

She and Bobby, both gearheads descended from gearheads, already had a '32 Ford Coupe and a replica of a '65 Shelby Cobra. But damn it, there was a vacancy in her life that could only be filled by ownership of a vintage truck.

She hadn't settled on the year and make lightly. Her focus had narrowed over countless trips to car shows, in which she and Bobby had seen a lot of models and years. For a number of reasons, 1941, the last full year of trucks before Ford had retooled itself into a war machine, was her favorite. The following year, 1942, Ford stopped production in February, resulting in a limited number of trucks that had grown exceedingly rare and expensive over the intervening decades. Besides, Ford had redesigned them to look less like the cars. A mistake, in Christine's opinion.

Once truck production started up again after World War II, Ford compounded the error by further redesigning the grill and fenders, resulting in a truck that had completely lost the art deco lines, which was what had attracted Christine to the earlier trucks in the first place.

1941 was the year. She was determined to make it happen.

A bit later, while at home changing into something decent, it occurred to her that her ankle had limbered up a little, and she barely felt it anymore. Evidently it wasn't that bad of a sprain. A little ibuprofen should take care of it. She hadn't even had a chance to ice it this morning, and now she figured she wouldn't bother.

After changing clothes, she picked two Janis O'Riordan hardbacks off her shelf and went to the kitchen. "Sure you don't wanna go with me?" she asked her husband.

"Book release party? No thanks," he said with a roll of his eyes.

Christine had been in love with Bobby since high school. They'd been attracted to each other for their shared love of music and auto mechanics, but reading wasn't a hobby they shared.

They'd been married for twenty years and were raising two young sons together. Bobby was a bit of a neat freak, which rankled her at times, but he made up for it in ways beyond counting. She'd learned to live with his quirks, just as she was sure he'd learned to live with hers, although that wasn't something she'd ever admit out loud.

"I had to ask," she said. "You three will be all right for dinner, right?"

"I was gonna make some spaghetti," he said as he

struggled to open a jar of Prego, "but maybe I'll just air-fry some chicken fingers."

Chris took the jar from him, popped it open without visible effort, and handed it back to him.

He looked at the jar, then looked at his wife. "I loosened it for you," he said.

"Right."

"Well, I did sprain my wrist today at the shop."

"Funny," she said. "I sprained my ankle today. What are the odds?"

"'Bout the same as the odds that you tripped over your own shoe because you were in such a hurry to get out the door."

She spent a heartbeat or three trying to figure out if he was agreeing with her or blaming her and decided it didn't matter. Her husband understood her like no other. He'd given her an out, and she took it. "So, anyway…"

"Anyway," he said, "don't worry about us. We'll be fine."

"Okay," she said with a smile. "See ya."

"And thanks for not killing me," he said.

"Maybe tomorrow," she said. "Bye, boys!" she yelled into the living room, where Kyle and Evan, their two sons, were playing video games.

"Bye, Mom!" they yelled in chorus.

Smiling, Christine bent to stroke her calico cat as it rubbed against her shin. "Keep the boys in line, Mrs. Jingles," she said. Straightening, she said to Bobby, "Don't—"

"—forget to feed the cat," he finished for her. "I got it. This ain't my first rodeo, you know."

She laughed and kissed him goodbye, the bristle of his goatee still giving her that flutter in her tummy, after all these years.

"You look nice," he said. "Have fun."

"Thanks. Maybe later …?"

Bobby smiled with one side of his mouth. "I don't know. I might be pretty worn out after all this noodle-boilin' and cat-feedin' I gotta do."

Christine laughed. "Love you," she said. She stepped out the door as he gave her the obligatory but heartfelt response.

She stepped back up into her Highlander and backed out of the driveway. It was a beautiful hot day in July, and she would have loved to take the '32 Coupe to park beside all the other classic cars that congregated at Double Groove. But evening thundershowers were in the forecast, and that was the end of the discussion. The Coupe would remain in the garage with the Shelby.

* * *

Five minutes later, she was back at the Groove. It was already after four o'clock and she could tell by the looks of the parking lot that things were considerably more hoppin' than they had been when she left. The lot in front of the ribbed-steel-sided former warehouse was full, and people were beginning to park on the street. The food truck had arrived. The deck outside the front doors was almost full of people, most clustered in the patches of shade cast by the sailcloths stretched overhead. She saw the Willig Boys, a local acoustic rock trio, setting up their equipment on the deck as well.

As she drove through the lot on her way to the back side of the building, where she customarily parked, she spotted Rick Rineer's pale yellow '67 Chevelle, chrome gleaming in the sun. Either he wasn't planning on staying long, or he hadn't checked the weather report. She made a mental note to bring it up when she ran into him.

She entered the brewhouse through the back door and went straight through to the taproom. When she opened the door, the air conditioning and the noise hit her at the same time. Dire Straits was playing, but Christine could barely hear it over the sounds of multiple conversations going on at the same time, each trying to outshout the others. Not quite like a Saturday night with Second Wind playing, but it was crowded. The taproom's legal capacity was seventy-five, and Christine figured it looked to be half to two-thirds full.

Double Groove's taproom was divided into two sides, the A-Side and the B-Side, in keeping with the vinyl record theme. The original taproom had been quite cozy, but when the Groove more than doubled its size after two years of business, the original room became the A-Side, and the expansion became the B-Side.

A long table and a lectern with a microphone were set up in the front corner of the A-Side, a couple of short chairs behind the table, and a barrel next to the lectern for use as a table. Janis O'Riordan stood behind the table, setting up some book displays. She was still pretty in her late fifties, blue-eyed, dark-haired, with a little bit of extra weight around her middle, and had reading glasses hanging around her neck. Christine recognized her as the slightly more aged version of the headshot that appeared on the inside flap of her dust jackets.

Helping Janis out was a tall man that looked vaguely familiar to Christine. He had a pleasantly square jaw and a hairline beginning to recede. He too looked to be in his mid-fifties, and Christine assumed it was Janis' husband, Brian Harrison. Working at Double Groove, she saw a lot of people, but she felt like that wasn't the reason she sort of recognized this particular gentleman. She'd seen him somewhere else. She couldn't suss it out on the spot, so she set it aside as some sort of déjà vu and moved on.

She thought about going up and introducing herself to Janis O'Riordan but decided against it. There'd be an opportunity later, and it might come more organically. *Be cool*, she thought. *Don't go all fangirl.* Besides, Janis seemed somehow aloof. The lack of a smile, the fact that she kept the tables between herself and everyone else, the way her eyes refused to settle on anyone, as if they didn't exist, all worked in tandem to say *Don't approach me.*

Christine shrugged. *Whatever.*

She caught Megan's eye behind the bar and waggled her fingers at her, got a smile and a wave back. Bartender Steven Kutcher, Janis' nephew, had arrived by this time; he had his back to Megan, pouring somebody a pint from the Atomic Blonde tap.

Over on the B-Side, Lisa Moody, Mark's wife and Double Groove's de facto CEO, was serving beers to the patrons at tables. She was their resident IT and social media guru, and a marketing whiz with a mind for numbers. The magnitude of her contribution in handling all the scheduling and accounting tasks for the business far exceeded her elfin stature.

But she still served beer. It was a small business and everybody pitched in.

Christine made her way to the bar and asked Megan, "You guys need any help back there?"

"Nah," Megan said. "We're doing fine for now, and Mark should be back soon. Enjoy yourself. Want a beer?"

"I'll take a Black Magic."

"You got it, honey."

As Megan ran Christine's card, Steven, thirty-three with dark hair and a goatee, picked up a glass and took it to the tap.

"AYYYYY!" came a loud male voice from behind Christine. She turned, expecting to find Fonzie, but instead saw a trim man of average height in a Double Groove tie-dye baseball cap entering the taproom. His arms extended wide, he met Janis O'Riordan and wrapped her in a bear hug. "Janis, baby!" he bellowed. "How've you been?"

"I'm fine, Scott," she answered with a pained smile. "And you?"

"Fantastic, baby, fantastic." Upon closer inspection, the man struck Christine as an older fellow trying to look young, and not doing a particularly good job of it. He was probably Janis' age or older. He had a couple of gold chains hanging behind his meticulously-ironed white shirt, and at least four bulky rings on his knobby fingers. A sharp crease was ironed into his tan slacks, and she bet that ball cap disguised the fact that his salt-and-pepper temples didn't exactly meet at the top.

Behind him stood a flip-lipped blonde woman in a tight minidress, watching the proceedings with a decidedly sour look on her face.

"Hey, anybody sitting right here?" Scott asked loyal patrons John and Sue Harris, who were sitting at the high table in front of the window. "Megan," he shouted as he and his sulking companion sat down without waiting for an answer, "put these fine folks' next beers on my tab, would ya? And a Mild Kinda Lover for Tina, and I'll take a Gimme Three Hops."

Christine turned back to face Megan. "Jesus," Megan said in a low voice that only Christine could hear, "I hate that guy."

"He been here before?"

"Yeah, a few times. He's friggin' obnoxious. Always comes in already plastered, thinks he owns the place."

"Seems like he knows Janis O'Riordan."

"Knows her? I heard he's her ex-husband. His name is Scott Cornell and Tina is his current arm ornament. I mean wife."

"You gonna get their beers?" Christine asked.

"Not till he brings his card over here," Megan said. "He used to be a brewer over at Chesapeake Brewery, so he thinks he's special."

"But he's not," both women said at the same time. Then they laughed and exchanged a fist bump.

"Great minds," Megan said.

Christine took a swig from her Black Magic, appreciating the crisp, clean taste with just a slight touch of lime flavor from the Motueka hops. She usually gravitated toward IPAs, but a hot afternoon like this sometimes benefited from a lager with a light mouthfeel like Black Magic. "You said '*used* to be a brewer'?" she said.

"Yeah. I heard he got in some kind of trouble over there and got fired. For selling their recipes, or something like that."

A dog growled behind Christine. As she started to turn, a shout came from Scott Cornell, and almost simultaneously, the dog yelped as if in pain. Christine finished turning in time to see the dog, a chocolate lab, running away from Scott, toward the B-Side with her tail between her legs.

"Oh my God, he just kicked that dog," Megan said.

"He bit me!" Scott said. "Well, he tried to. He tore my pants, look!"

Christine knew the dog. Her name was Honey, despite Scott's confusion about her gender. Honey was high-spirited like most chocolates, but she would never snap at anyone unless she felt threatened or cornered. At the moment, she was all lolling tongue and furiously wagging tail as she received some love and comfort from her humans.

Christine could tell Honey's humans, a local veterinarian and his wife, were irritated with Scott, as Dad cast a withering glare in Scott's direction. But if the dog's owners were perturbed, Lisa, standing nearby, was a four-foot-eleven picture of perfect rage. Her face was almost purple, her fists were clenched, and Christine could swear she saw a vein pulsing in Lisa's forehead.

Christine moved toward Lisa, and Steven came from behind the bar to join her. "You didn't see what happened, did you?" he said to Lisa.

"No. But I can guess."

"Don't throw him out," he said. "He's a jerk, and I'm not exactly proud of him, but he was my uncle once. The thing is, if you chuck him, Aunt Janis might go with him."

And if she leaves, Christine thought, *so will half the people in this taproom,* a detail that that would factor into Lisa's decision very little, if at all.

Lisa stared at Steven, then shifted her gaze to Christine.

"He's right," Christine said. "Leave it go for now."

"He's lucky Mark's not here," Lisa said. "When he gets back, then we'll see. In the meantime, Mr. Pretty Boy better not cause any more trouble." She pushed between Steven and Christine and marched back into the brewhouse.

Steven watched her disappear, a pensive frown on his face.

"She's just going to cool off," Christine said. "She'll be okay."

Steven nodded wordlessly and went around the table to talk to his former uncle the troublemaker, while Christine stepped back to continue her conversation with Megan.

"See what I mean?" Megan said.

Christine let a breath out through puffed cheeks. "Yup." Then, as if they needed something else to worry about, she happened to glance out the window, and spotted a familiar red beard outside, ambling over toward the food truck. "Oh, great," she said. "He's back."

"Who?"

Christine pointed. "Keith Bonham."

CHAPTER THREE

AS BONHAM CONTINUED walking, Christine pulled her phone from her hip pocket and snapped a picture of him, just in case, right before he got at the end of the food truck line and turned his back to her.

"Whatcha lookin' at there, Chris?" burly, crew-cutted, and recently retired Rick Rineer said.

"Just this guy out there that Mark kicked out earlier. No big deal."

The front door opened, and the sound of the Willig Boys doing their sound check flooded the room. Along with the music, Mike Strazzire, a former Marine who only cut his flowing dark hair when it grew long enough that he could donate it to children with cancer, came in. Following Strazz, Christine saw another regular, Regis Burke, and then tall, thin Jerry McKernan. Jerry was Double Groove's landlord, and also the proprietor of Not Just Vacs, the sewing machine and vacuum cleaner repair shop that occupied the other half of the building.

Megan waved. "Hey, Jerry," she said. Megan had worked at Not Just Vacs for years before taking the job at Double Groove and now worked both jobs. Jerry was her boss on some days, but not today.

The door started to close, then yet another regular, mustachioed Randy Frey, entered. Finally the door closed behind them, and the album spinning on the turntable again took over.

Regis joined the Rineers and the Harrises, who had moved to the Rineers' table to get away from Scott. Strazz, Jerry, and Randy walked past Christine and disappeared into the B-Side somewhere.

"Hey, Regis," she said. "How are ya?"

"Looking forward to meeting this author," he said. Like Christine, Regis numbered reading among his hobbies, as did Sue Harris.

"By the way," Christine said, turning back to Rick, "you know it's supposed to rain tonight, right?"

"Yeah, I know," Rick said. "But it won't be until late. We're gonna get out of here around eight. Why'n'cha sit down with us?"

"I believe I will."

"Hey," Stella Rineer said as Christine pulled out a stool, "is that the guy you were talking about right there? The one Mark threw out?"

Chris followed Stella's blue-eyed gaze. "Yeah, that's him. Why? You know him?"

"No, but I know he's trouble. I went to high school with his wife. I wouldn't say she and I are close, but we're Facebook friends."

"How's it going, Mark?" Rick said.

Christine turned to see her smiling boss approaching from behind her.

"Livin' the dream," Mark said, his stock answer. Then, to Christine, "Hey, Viking. Did you kill him?" His eyes glittered with mirth.

"Huh? Kill who?" Christine said.

"Your husband."

"Oh. No, I decided to keep him."

"Because ...," he said while gesturing for her to continue.

"Because I'm fond of him."

"And whose fault was it that you sprained your ankle?"

"Well ... I mean, it's not exactly clear."

Mark threw back his head laughing.

"What's so funny?"

"Bobby's a neat freak. I bet you a beer he didn't leave his shoe in the doorway."

"Oh, shut up."

Mark laughed again, and Christine's tablemates joined him. "You can't do it," he said.

"Can't do what?"

"Admit you were wrong."

"Can we change the subject, please? Did anybody tell you about this guy Scott over here?"

Mark's expression sobered in an eyeblink. "Yeah, Lisa gave me a heads up on the way through the brewhouse. I'm gonna have a talk with him. I'm not gonna disrupt this event by throwing him out, but I'm leaning toward banning him starting tomorrow, depending on what he says to me."

"Okay, good. Also, I wanted to make sure you know Keith Bonham is back. He's right out there." She pointed, but Bonham had disappeared. Again. "Well, he *was* just there."

"Damn." He paused for thought. "Okay, as long as he stays out there, I won't make an issue of that, either. He can go to the food truck or sit at the picnic tables or whatever. But I don't want him on the deck, and for God's sake don't anybody serve him any beer. Keep an eye on him if you can, and let me know if he does anything stupid."

"Lot going on tonight," Rick said.

"For sure," Mark said. "So, you guys got this?"

"Got it," Christine said.

"Yep," Rick said. "Consider it handled, buddy."

"All right. I'll handle the dog-kicker."

Mark left them. Christine took a sip of her Mexican lager and people-watched for a while.

Looking around, she saw a taproom chock full of people, predominantly Gen-Xers, all mildly buzzed, talking and laughing, as it should be. She knew a good many by name. She noticed that Sheriff Alan Curtis had left by this time, as was his habit, but Deputy Ronnie Gaines still occupied the seat at the end of the bar where he'd been earlier today, talking to a couple of people she didn't know. *He must be about four beers deep by this time*, she thought. *He'd better be careful.*

She'd have to remember to steer clear of that area. Ronnie had gotten a little flirty with her from time to time, and it made her uncomfortable. The rest of the staff had made it clear they all thought she was overreacting, but Christine had been around long enough to know when a man was signaling interest.

Turning back to the front, she saw the hulking but harmless Mikey Karavas wrapped up in friendly—*very* friendly, judging by the tattooed arm he'd wrapped around her waist—conversation with a young woman, busty and flaunting it. Christine considered it a near certainty Mikey was *not* here for the book release party. When Mikey, also known as Stumpgrinder, came to Double Groove, he was looking for a connection. Of the female variety. Christine shook her head in resigned amusement. *Men.*

She felt a nudge at her ankle, and she looked down to find Honey, staring up at her with an expectant look. Christine dutifully ruffled the dog's ears with a smile, and

Honey moved on. She really was a sweet dog. Christine and Bobby had never owned a dog, but sometimes she wondered if it might be time …

Looking up again, Christine noticed Mark, already having a serious conversation with Scott Cornell. She found it amusing that, at first glance, the two men, who couldn't be more different, looked like they could almost be brothers. *Wonder how that discussion's going?* she thought. From the peaceful but stern look on Mark's face, and the fact that Scott kept nodding, it was at least civilized. One thing, maybe, that she didn't have to worry about anymore.

Christine happened to look at Janis O'Riordan then, and it was a good thing, because if she hadn't, she would have missed the whole thing. Janis and her husband Brian—who still seemed annoyingly familiar—were engaged in a heated discussion of their own. Then Brian raised a hand as if to touch Janis on the shoulder, but she smacked it away and turned her back on him, leaving Brian to glance furtively around the room to see if anyone was watching. He caught Christine's eye and she gave him a weak smile, trying to convey her sympathy across the crowded room. He waved, then he shrugged as if to say, "What can I do?" and turned away to unpack books from the box behind him.

Christine shook her head ruefully. Tensions were running high tonight. She had a small FoMO moment as she realized things were happening on all sides of her, and there was no way she could take it all in at once.

Her thoughts drifted back to that little wave from Brian. Had he recognized her? Later, if the opportunity presented itself, she should speak to him and find out if he could help her dispel the mystery of how they knew each other.

A glimpse of flame-red hair distracted her from that thought, and she turned to see that Amy Willig, a habitual social wanderer and the wife of the Willig Boys' lead singer,

Jeff, had cornered Strazz, and she was tasting his beer. Christine smiled. *Some things never change.*

"Uh-oh," Sue Harris said. Christine turned to face her, and Sue inclined her head toward Scott Cornell with a lift of her eyebrows.

Mark was gone, but now Brian and Scott, Janis' ex- and current husband, were face-to-face, gesticulating angrily at each other almost as if they might come to blows.

Christine sighed. Why did there have to be so much drama tonight? Just as she was about to run and find Mark again, the two men separated. Scott sat down and Brian went back behind the table with his wife, who ignored him.

It seemed everybody in the O'Riordan party was mad at everybody else in the O'Riordan party. If they got through this evening without any major blowups, it would be a miracle. Christine began to wish she'd stayed home.

She looked around for Mark but didn't see him, so she excused herself from the table and made a trip to the bathroom. From the hallway in front of the bathrooms, she could see into the brewhouse through the glass door, but she saw no sign of Mark in there, either. She wanted to make sure he knew about what she'd just seen go on between Brian and Scott and figured she'd look for him when she finished her business.

When she came out of the bathroom, she found Steven entertaining patrons at one of the low tables against the wall. Steven, when he wasn't serving beer or playing the drums, was an accomplished magician, and had given several magic shows at Double Groove. His shows always drew a huge crowd.

Christine stopped to watch. In the background, she finally found Mark, now talking to Janis and Brian. It seemed like he was about to get behind the microphone and start the proceedings.

Meanwhile, Steven was doing a card trick Christine had seen before, although it never failed to amaze. "I don't know if you knew this," he said to his audience, "but the way magicians work is they can go back in time and change things." His crowd laughed good-naturedly.

"It's true," Steven said as he fanned out a deck of cards face up so everyone could see it had the normal assortment of diamonds, clubs, hearts, and spades, then he turned it over and started passing cards from his right hand to his left, one at a time. "I'm gonna go through this deck like this, you tell me when to stop." After a dozen cards or so, a woman told him to stop, and he handed her what was then the top card in his right hand. Then he repeated the process and gave the woman a second card. "Now I'm gonna prove to you that I traveled in time," he said.

Christine knew the two cards the woman had chosen would be the four of spades and the eight of hearts, the same as the two cards Steven had tattooed on the deltoid muscle of his left arm. What she hadn't yet figured out was how he did it. He was about to ask the woman to expose her cards, then he would show her that he'd gone back in time and tattooed them on his arm. Ooh, ahh.

"Stupid trick," said Scott, as he elbowed his way past Steven to get to the bathrooms. "He's had that tattoo for eight years, and he's peeling the cards off the bottom of the deck."

Christine's jaw dropped at his off-the-charts rudeness, and so did those of the spectators.

"Why would you do that?" Steven said to Scott, looking like he was ready to jump down his ex-uncle's throat.

Scott only laughed and continued on his way past the table, past Christine, and into the bathroom.

"I'm gonna kill him," Steven said. "Feckin eejit."

"It's okay," one of the women at the table said. "Show

us the rest of the trick."

Steven, thrown off his game, fought to recover his mojo and finished the trick, even though the effect was somewhat blunted. His audience was polite enough to act astonished.

"Everybody, can I have your attention?" Mark said over the microphone.

CHAPTER FOUR

FROM BEHIND THE bar, Megan turned off the music, and voices on the A-Side quieted. It took a repeated call for attention to silence the B-Side.

"Hey, everybody," Mark continued. "Thanks for coming tonight. Here at Double Groove, we like to support our local businesses and talent. As most of you know, we're here tonight to celebrate the release of the latest book by our favorite local author, Janis O'Riordan."

There was polite applause. Janis nodded her head, smiled, and waved.

"Janis is the author of almost twenty books, most of them cozy mysteries," Mark continued. "I know a lot of you already know this, but she's a brilliant writer. I've read her myself, and I don't pass out that kind of praise lightly, but hey, don't take it from me. She's already won two Agatha Awards and an Edgar, so she's the real deal. We're honored to be able to have her here, and if you haven't read any of her work, do yourself a favor.

"Tonight she's gonna give us a free preview of her brand new book that comes out tomorrow, and then she'll answer any questions you might have."

"Any?" someone in the crowd said.

"Within reason! We also have copies of the latest book up here for sale, and yes, it's a day early. I'm sure if you're nice you might be able to talk her into signing a copy. We also have an assortment of some of her earlier titles. So without further ado, I present ... Janis O'Riordan."

"Thank you," Janis said as she took the lectern. She waited for the applause to die down, then said, "Can everybody hear me? Yes? Good.

"You may have heard," she continued, "that most writers are introverts, and I'm no exception, so this is a little out of my wheelhouse. With that in mind, I'm going to go straight into the reading. Ready?"

She picked up a copy of her latest mystery, *Pie to Die For*, and opened it to the first page. "'It was a dark and stormy night,'" she began.

Silence.

Christine looked around the room and saw jaws had fallen open, and a few people winced openly. She heard one "Holy crap" spoken under someone's breath, which, in the stillness of the room, rang out like a shout.

"Just kidding," Janis said. "Gotcha."

The room erupted into relieved laughter. Christine looked around the room to watch and saw Amy Willig, one of Double Groove's unofficial photographers, busily snapping pics of the laughing faces with her phone.

Janis' perfect comedic timing had served to break the ice, and perhaps settle her own nerves. When she went into the actual reading, her voice was clear, strong, and emotive, her pacing steady but unrushed. The room was rapt. Outside of a select few editors, beta readers, and family members, the fans gathered here were the first people to hear these words, and Christine keenly felt the privilege.

A hush fell over the taproom as Janis closed the book.

"I'll take some questions now."

At first it seemed no one had the nerve to speak up, and Christine was in the process of raising her hand when Regis Burke rescued her. "How do you come up with so many ways to kill people without getting caught?"

Janis laughed. "I mean, all of my murderers, without exception, do get caught, so…"

"Well, if it weren't for your sleuths, a lot of them might not have," Regis said, smiling.

"So what you're asking me, essentially, is how to commit a perfect murder, right? Is there anyone in your life we need to worry about?"

When the subsequent hilarity died down, Regis expounded on his question. "I mean, as a writer, where do you get your ideas? How do you research how to pull off a perfect murder?"

"Okay," Janis said. "That's a good question. In the old days, I used to read the papers a lot. I talked to police officers, I read true crime stories and watched them on TV. And then of course, *CSI* came out, and there was *Dateline*, et cetera."

Christine was momentarily distracted by fierce whispering to her left, and she glanced over to see Scott and Tina Cornell bickering under their breath.

"And I would take little ideas from each story," Janis continued, "and kind of twist them around and recombine them for my own stories. Nowadays, of course, there's the Internet, and that makes it really easy, although I do worry about my search history—" She mimicked typing on a keyboard and said in her best Bela Lugosi imitation, "'How to commit a perfect murder.'"

Scott rose from his seat and crossed in front of the lectern to go to the bar. A flicker of irritation crossed Janis' face, but she played it off well. "So don't do that," she said, "unless you fancy a couple of suits in dark sunglasses at your door." This was met with more laughter.

As another fan asked a question of Janis, Scott wobbled up to the bar and summoned Megan with the crook of a finger.

Christine finished her beer, rose from her seat, and walked over to stand behind Scott in line.

"What can I get for you?" Megan said to Scott.

"Bang Your Hops, please."

Megan went to the tap and pulled a pint for Scott, then brought it to him. Behind Christine, Janis was cheerily answering the latest question as if nothing else was going on.

"What's thish?" Scott said. "This isn't Gimme Three Hops, I can tell by the color. What are you tryin' to pull on me, girl? You think I'm stuhhh-stupid?"

"You asked for Bang Your Hops."

"I very clearly asked for Gimme She Hops. Three Hops. Did you just roll your eyes at me?"

"No, I—"

"You did. You rolled your eyes. Is that any way to treat a loyal cushtomer?"

"I'm sorry, I must have misunderstood you. I'll get you a Gimme Three Hops."

"Well, make it snappy," he said, snapping his fingers in Megan's face three times. "I don't have all fu—"

"HEY!" Megan shouted in his face. "Don't you ever—"

"Megan," said Mark, who had appeared like magic behind her, "go take a break. And you," he said to Scott in a firm but quiet voice, "are cut off. You need to lower your voice and go back to your seat. Did you forget the deal we made earlier?"

Scott paused, his reddened eyes assuming a thousand-mile stare as Christine watched, and she realized he was trying to remember exactly what had gone between him and Mark. Then he said, "Yeah, okay."

Christine watched Scott turn, walk back to his table, and sit down.

Janis, who had paused to watch the end of the drama, continued with her answer. Her face was visibly flushed, but only those closest to the action had any idea that anything had happened at all. Mark had somehow managed to avert a spectacle.

Immediate crisis over, Christine decided to check on Megan, who easily took offense, and particularly loathed it when people snapped their fingers in command. She went into the empty brewhouse to find her friend stomping around hurling curses at the walls, her face a contorted mask of rage.

"You okay?" Christine asked.

"Am I okay? What do you think? Did you see the way that guy treated me? I could friggin' kill him. *Nobody* snaps their fingers at me like that! Oooh, I just wanna *scream*!"

"So do it."

"What? Scream?" Megan said.

"Yeah, it might do you good. Scream therapy, it's a thing, believe it or not."

"What the—are you kidding me?"

"No, it's for real," Christine said. "There's actual research. Endorphins or something."

Megan smiled, then drew in a huge breath and opened her mouth.

"Not here, dummy!" Christine said. "You want everyone to think you're being murdered back here? Go outside and do it."

"But I can't just…"

"I'll cover for you," Christine said. "You want to do it, I can tell. So go."

Megan nodded. "Yeah. I might. I'll sit in my car so people don't hear it."

Christine nodded. "Go. I got you."

"Thanks, Chris." And with that, Megan turned and exited the brewhouse through the back door.

Christine sighed and went back behind the bar to take over for Megan. She glanced at the clock. It was five-forty, with the Q&A session still chugging merrily along. The Willig Boys were scheduled to start their set at six, and she hoped the questions would grind to a halt soon so there'd be no conflict.

As she took an order from a patron, she snuck a peek at Scott Cornell to make sure he was behaving and caught him digging in his pants pocket. He extracted his phone and held it at heart level to look at the screen. From the way his eyes flicked back and forth, she assumed he was reading a text.

She ran the patron's card, and as she handed it back to him, she saw Scott heading back the hallway toward the bathrooms. *Good,* she thought. *At least while he's in the john, he's not getting into trouble.* She pulled the patron's beer and took it back to him.

And speaking of trouble, where had Brian gotten to? He was no longer behind the book-laden table with his wife.

The Q&A session went on without further interruption. Even Janis, who had clearly been embarrassed, seemed to be enjoying herself.

After a half hour, the questions finally ran out, and Mark moved again to the lectern to announce the end of the session and the opening up of book sales. Steven started the music again, and conversation swelled as Janis O'Riordan fans lined up to buy copies of her latest book, speak to her, and get her to sign their books.

The Willig Boys, who had delayed their set by ten

minutes so as not to interfere with the indoor proceedings, started their first number. Some patrons began wandering outside to listen.

Janis sat behind the table, chatting it up with fans and signing books with a writerly flourish, without any help or support from her missing husband. Tina Cornell had vanished as well, and Scott, the fourth and final member of the Dysfunctional Four, had yet to return from the bathroom. Was he having a baby in there?

"Megan still on break?" Mark asked, breaking into her thoughts.

"Yeah, I told her to go for a walk outside," Christine said, unwilling to share the actual details of her discussion with Megan. "I'm covering for her."

"It's been a while."

"I'll go look for her," Lisa said. "Be right back."

Lisa disappeared into the brewhouse, and Christine asked a patron with an empty glass if she needed a refill.

A scream ripped through the air.

"Lisa?" Mark said, turning his head toward the production area.

Christine, who was closer to the brewhouse than Mark, dropped her glass in the sink and ran to the brewhouse door. She burst through it and found Lisa standing with her hands on her face.

"Get Ronnie!" Lisa said. Behind her was the body of a man, face down on the floor, next to the stairs that led up to the loft over the taproom. A trail of smeared blood ran across the room, from the man's head to the soapstone ledge surrounding the trench drain.

For a brief instant, despite the fact that she'd just left Mark at the bar, Christine's heart thudded in her chest as her eyes told her that her boss was somehow lying motionless on the floor before her, with a trail of blood running from his face. But as she moved past Lisa, she realized the resemblance to Mark was superficial, and only from behind, and even then, only with the hat on. Once she had a clear view of the injured man's face and balding crown, it became apparent that it wasn't Mark at all.

It was Scott Cornell.

CHAPTER FIVE

CHRISTINE KNELT TO check for a pulse, but when she saw Scott's face, she realized there was no need. The pressure of his cheek resting on the floor had pinched his left eye almost completely closed, but his lifeless right eye was wide open, staring at nothing. His mangled lips and broken nose had stopped bleeding.

He was dead.

Mark, thankfully very much alive, entered the room. Christine looked up at him and said, "Tell Ronnie."

"Shit," Mark said, and he darted back into the taproom.

"Did somebody stab him?" Lisa said.

"I don't think so," Christine said. "There's not enough blood. I think what blood there is came from his nose or his mouth, or both."

"Maybe he fell, then," Lisa said. "It looks like he might've hit the ledge here, where his hat's lying."

"He might have fallen and hit his face there," Christine said, "but I think somebody helped him fall. They pushed him, or hit him with something. See this trail, where his face dragged from the ledge to here? I don't think he crawled backwards with his face on the floor, do you?

Somebody dragged him by the feet, and he was already dead, or at least unconscious. They probably moved him because of that door right there." Christine pointed, indicating the door to the taproom.

"Yeah," Lisa said. "Anybody going to the bathrooms could've seen him lying there where he first fell."

"Exactly."

Lisa shuddered. "So the killer's still here somewhere."

Christine paused, thinking. "Maybe. There's always the back door."

Ronnie Gaines came through the taproom door, Mark right behind him. "Christine, get away from him," Ronnie said. "Nobody touch anything. I'm calling 9-1-1. I've been drinking, so somebody else needs to respond. Did anybody touch that hat?"

"No," Christine said as she moved to stand with Mark and Lisa.

"Good. There's blood on the bill, I can see that from here."

"What could they have hit him with?" Lisa said.

"Anything," Mark said. "There's tons of—" He froze, staring at the wall over the canning machine. "The transfer pipe's missing."

"What's that?" Ronnie said.

"Bulldog pipe. Fourteen-gauge stainless steel, about four feet long, with a short L at the end. It was definitely there earlier today."

Ronnie nodded. "They'll find it. Meantime, everybody out of here. This room is now a crime scene." He dug his phone out and dialed 9-1-1.

Mark, Lisa, and Christine went back into the taproom, where things were proceeding as if nothing had happened.

"I gotta hit the ladies' room," Christine said. She stepped inside, closed the door, and extracted her phone from her hip pocket to call Megan. She started to make the call, then reconsidered and decided to use FaceTime instead. "Where are you?" she said in a hushed voice when Megan's face appeared on the screen.

"In my car, can't you tell? And you're in the bathroom. Hey, you were right, you know. It really works. Screaming, I mean. I feel so much better."

Christine was happy to get visual corroborative evidence that Megan was, indeed, in her car. "Get back in here now. Don't use the back door, come in through the taproom. Something's happened."

"What—"

"Just get in here, and don't tell anybody where you were."

"Okay, I'm coming."

"Wait."

"What? I thought you were in a hurry."

"Megan," Christine said with hesitation, "you didn't do anything crazy, did you?"

"I mean, screaming by yourself in your car ... I guess that could be considered crazy, but—"

Christine shook her head violently. "There's a dead guy back there, in the brewhouse."

Megan's hand flew to her mouth. "A dead guy? What happened?"

"Megan ... it's Scott Cornell."

Christine watched Megan's expression morph from one of horror to one of pitiless mirth. "Hah! Are you kidding me? Well, it couldn't have happened to a nicer fella, that's all I got to say."

"Megan!"

"Sorry. I know it's messed up somebody died in the brewhouse, but he was an ass—"

"Megan! Shut up, will you? He didn't just die. He was

murdered."

Megan shut up. "Oh," she said in a quiet voice.

"Yeah. That's why I asked you ..."

"Oh, I see. You thought I did something *really* crazy."

"I mean, I had to ask. Another thing. Do you know where the bulldog pipe is?"

"You mean it's not hanging on the wall?"

"It's not," Christine said.

"How should I know then?"

Christine gusted out a breath, satisfied from seeing Megan's reaction that she was innocent. She felt a tad guilty for doubting her friend even for a second, but Megan *was* ... volatile. It had to be ruled out. "Just get in here, okay? I'll meet you at the door."

Christine left the bathroom and walked to the front door, arriving just as Megan got there from outside. She opened the door for Megan to enter, glancing around to see how many people had noticed. A few, but none seemed interested, and Ronnie Gaines, who was still in the brewhouse, was not among them. That was all that mattered.

"Get in there behind the bar and act like you were never gone," Christine said. "Hear me?"

Megan nodded. "Gotcha."

As Megan worked the bar with Steven, Mark went outside with Ronnie, and Christine trailed along with them. The Willig Boys were playing "Stuck in the Middle With You." Christine finally found Brian Harrison, who'd been missing for the last half hour or so, sitting at a table with two other men, right in front of the band. Maybe he'd been there all along, maybe not. He was in a location she would not have been able to see from her earlier position inside.

Seconds later, a Sheriff's Office Ford Explorer screeched into the parking lot and disgorged Lieutenant George

Booker, another Double Groove regular who had been friends with Sheriff Curtis for decades. He spit out a broken toothpick and met Mark, Ronnie, and Christine on the deck.

"Hey, Book," Mark said. "Anything I can do to help?"

Booker nodded. "Help me herd all those people out at the picnic tables over here onto the deck, then get back inside. I'll be out here, keeping an eye on everybody and taking down license plates in case anybody decides to leave before I can stop 'em."

Mark nodded. "Sheriff coming?"

"He's already here, out back. The CI team should be here any minute, and they're gonna lock the place down. Nobody in, nobody out. Until they interview everybody."

"Everybody?"

"Every last one."

"That could take hours."

Booker nodded. "A lot of 'em will only have to give names and phone numbers, so not as long as you might think, but yeah. Also, just so you know, the Forensics team will be processing the crime scene in the back and the M.E. will process the body and then take it away. He or she will get here later, maybe an hour or so. They had to call one in from Baltimore."

"Damn," Mark said.

"You got anywhere in there we could talk to people in private?"

"I would have said the brewhouse, but there's a body in there. So other than that, not much. The bathrooms. The cold room, which is … cold."

"Hmm."

"Hey, hold on, I got it. You can use next door." Mark pointed to the former location of White Tiger Distillery, a single-bay business that had once occupied the end of the building opposite Not Just Vacs, with Double Groove sandwiched between them. Double Groove now controlled that bay. They used it for storage, and occasionally for pop-up shops around the holidays.

"That's perfect," George said. "And you may as well close the bar now, Mark. No more drinking. We're all in for a long night."

Mark, dejected but resigned, went to the picnic tables to start redirecting people to the deck. The Willig Boys finished their song, and Jeff, having noticed the fuss, said over the mic with a smiling face, "Anything we should know?"

George wandered over to Jeff and spoke quietly to him, off mic. Jeff did some nodding, then turned to his brother Blaise, sitting on the cajón, and bass player Joe Wilson to relay what he'd learned from George. Then he came back to the mic and said, "We're gonna do one more song, folks, then take a break." Then they launched into the Jeff Willig original "Hangin' Out at Double Groove," a number that always got the crowd singing along.

"Hangin' out with friends, the party never ends, it's a blast," Jeff sang.

> *We don't want it to be done,*
> *But you know when you're havin' fun,*
> *The time goes fast*
> *We've got quite a crew*
> *Hangin' out at Double Groove.*

As the song continued, Christine, smiling despite the situation at hand, wandered back inside, then she called Bobby and gave him the bad news.

"Want me to come over?" he asked.

"No. They won't let you in anyway. Hopefully I'll get out

of here in time to get some sleep. I'd still like to go to Elkton and look at that truck in the morning." They'd found a decent-looking truck on the Internet a couple of days ago, for a good price, and had arranged with the owner to see it the next day. Christine didn't want to miss it.

"Yeah, that would be best," Bobby said. "It might not be there for long. Keep me posted."

"Will do." She hung up with her husband and sat back at the table with the Rineers and the Harrises, where they waited to see what would happen next. Mark and Lisa went to sit at another table.

"I'm so glad I didn't have to see that," Steven said as he and Megan joined Christine's table. "Pretty sure I would've thrown up."

"Yeah," Christine said with a smile, "you would've." Steven's squeamishness was a frequent magnet for good-natured derision at Double Groove. The sight of any bodily fluid made him gag.

Christine watched as the word spread that the bar was closed and that they all might be forbidden to leave. A range of expressions moved across the room like a wave. Sadness, shock, concern, annoyance, and anger were all on full display. There were even a few who, talking and laughing, had evidently either not yet heard about the murder or decided they were going to have fun no matter what. Janis was crying, arms wrapped around Brian, who had come back inside to join her in the front corner. Tina Cornell, Scott's widow, was still nowhere to be seen. Had they maybe let her in the back to be with her husband's body?

Outside, the Willig Boys finished their song and went directly into the load out.

This party was over.

The Criminal Investigations team soon arrived and took charge of the situation. Two of them marched into the brewhouse, and minutes later, Alan Curtis, now in uniform and with his mouth set in a grim line, came out from the brewhouse and went behind the lectern.

"Can I get everyone's attention please?" he said, raising his voice. Once the crowd settled down, he continued. "Thank you. I'm Sheriff Alan Curtis … most of y'all already know that, although ya might notta seen me in uniform before."

Polite laughter bounced around the room as Alan smiled.

"I'm sure y'all've heard by now," he continued, "that there's been a crime committed here tonight. That means nobody leaves until I say so." The smile had vanished.

Groans came from the crowd. Despite the fact that most everyone assembled had already heard this bruited about, it hadn't become real until it came from Alan's mouth.

"Now, I'm sorry about this," Alan said, "but it's gotta be done. We'll try to sort things out as quick as we can so y'all can get back to your homes and families, and the more cooperation we get from y'all, the faster this'll go, you foller me? I know mosta y'all, and I know y'all are good people, and I don't expect there to be no problems. Now, right soon a fella from the Criminal Investigation unit is gonna set up next door, and he'll be callin' you folks over there one at a time to talk to you each in private. In the meantime, I don't want ya to get offended, because we're all friends here, but we're gonna start separatin' certain people from each other, and I don't wanna see nobody using their cell phones. I'll be standin' right here. Foller me?"

The patrons greeted this with silence. This was getting *really* real. *Too* real.

"Excuse me a minute," Alan said. He stepped to the door and beckoned George Booker to come inside and join him. He spoke briefly to Booker in a quiet voice while Booker nodded, then Booker went back out and relayed to those on the deck what Alan had just explained to the taproom, then Booker and another deputy who had just arrived took up positions at the entrances to the deck, preventing anyone from leaving.

Christine and the others in the taproom cast nervous glances at each other. It was a frightening situation, and Christine felt a growing sense of dread. A nervous knot appeared in her abdomen. She knew she hadn't done anything illegal, and certainly hadn't killed anyone, but the secret she shared with Megan could be construed, if it came out, as impeding the investigation.

And yet, they had no option. If it became known that Megan had been AWOL during that time, she would instantly become a person of interest in a crime Christine knew she had not committed. Christine preferred that the cops focus on finding the actual killer, rather than waste time following up on an innocent person.

Especially if that innocent person was her friend.

Christine caught Megan's eye, and although no words were exchanged, she could tell Megan's mind was going through the same chain of logic. In a show of solidarity, Christine reached over and covered Megan's hand with her own. Megan smiled, her lips quivering just a bit. She was nervous, too.

A man wearing khakis and a plaid shirt under a blue blazer came from the brewhouse into the taproom and spoke to Mark, who handed him a set of keys. He then went to join Alan at the lectern. He was beefy in a rounded kind of way, and appeared to be in his mid-forties.

"This is Detective Kingery," Alan said. "He'll be callin'

y'all real soon."

Kingery nodded, then without a word, left via the front door, presumably to set up shop in the warehouse next door.

Over the next few minutes, the taproom grew quiet as voices gradually fell and the gravity of the situation settled on each patron at his or her own rate. The tension in the room seemed to build until Christine felt it must soon reach the bursting point, so that when the detective finally came back to the door and invited the first witness to come with him, it felt like the fall of a guillotine.

"Lisa Moody?" he said.

Lisa raised her hand. "Right here."

"Come with me, please." He held the door for her as she rose from her stool and exited the taproom, alone.

A soft muttering arose in the room as people released a collective held breath and, under the sheriff's watchful eye, began to talk softly to each other again.

Lisa's interview took about fifteen minutes, and when she came back to the taproom, Alan directed her to a table by herself, and Mark went next, like a tag team.

After another quarter hour, Mark came back and the detective said, "Christine Buckley?"

CHAPTER SIX

CHRISTINE LEFT HER seat and preceded the detective through the taproom door, and she noticed a breeze had picked up outside. She stopped to let Kingery pass her, then she followed him down the sidewalk to the former White Tiger door. The detective held the door for her, and she entered.

"Take a seat, please," he said, indicating a plastic chair on one side of a common folding six-foot table. She sat, and the detective walked around the table and sat opposite her. He had heavy eyelids, dark thinning hair combed straight back, and a pouty unsmiling mouth.

Christine wiped her sweaty palms on her pants, then extended her right hand across the table and introduced herself. "Christine," she said.

He nodded as he gave her hand a limp shake. "Kingery."

"And your first name is …?"

"Detective."

Yikes, Christine thought. Her first tentative attempt to establish a connection, rebuffed with prejudice. This was not going to be easy. Or fun.

After getting Christine's full name and address, Kingery asked his first real question.

"You were one of the first ones in the room with the

body, correct?"

"Yes. The second, actually." *Well, third, if you count the killer,* she thought but didn't say.

"Tell me how that happened."

"I was working behind the bar with Mark and Steven and I heard Lisa scream ... we all did. But I was the closest to the brewhouse door, so I ran in to see what was the matter. I found Lisa in there with ... the body."

"Where was she in relation to the body?"

"The body was ... where it is now, I guess, next to the stairs, and Lisa was at the foot of the stairs. Facing the door, headed toward me, I think."

"You think?"

"Well, she was definitely facing me. Whether she was moving before I got there, I can't be sure. I had the impression that she had just stopped moving when she heard me come through the door."

Kingery nodded as he wrote in his notepad. His expression was all business, and it made Christine nervous just looking at him.

"Has anything been moved or touched since you first saw the body?" he asked.

"I have no idea."

He looked up at her. "I mean between the time you got there and the time you left, was anything moved or touched? The body or anything else."

"No, not to my knowledge." She found that she didn't know what to do with her hands, and settled for folding them in front of her on the table.

"When was the last time you saw Scott Cornell alive?"

"*That* I can answer. The Q&A ended about six-ten, I know because the Willig Boys were supposed to have started at six, but the Q&A ran over, and I was steady looking at the clock. And about a half hour before the

Q&A ended, I saw Scott read something on his phone, then he went to … what I thought was the bathrooms at the time, but maybe he went straight to the brewhouse. I don't know."

"So … approximately five-forty was when you last saw him alive, correct?"

She double-checked his math in her head. "Yeah, that seems about right."

Kingery nodded. "You said he was looking at his phone when you last saw him?"

"Yes."

"Do you know where that phone might be now?"

"I would have said it's in his pocket, but I assume you've looked there already?"

Kingery stared at her.

"Then I don't know." *Wow*, she thought. *The phone's gone. I bet the killer took it.*

"Before today, had you ever met Mr. Cornell?"

"No."

"Can you account for your own whereabouts between five-forty and six-ten?"

"I told you. I was working behind the bar."

"Any witnesses that can corroborate that?"

"Mark and Steven. And about, I don't know, forty or fifty other people?"

"And who is Steven?"

"Kutcher. He works here."

Kingery nodded. "Do you know if Mr. Cornell had any enemies?" he asked.

"I mean, how much time do you have? He was obnoxious from the clutch-drop."

"Clutch-drop?" he asked from under those heavy eyelids.

"It's a figure of speech."

"Meaning he was obnoxious from the moment he entered the room?"

"You got it," she said.

"In what way?"

"He was already drunk when he got here. Loud, clumsy, arrogant, rude to people …"

"Rude to whom?"

Ah. The money question. Careful, now. "Well, his ex-wife, for starters."

"That would be Janis O'Riordan?"

"Yes. Also, his current wife looked angry with him, like maybe they'd been arguing on the way here." She ticked off Scott's victims on her fingers, this being the second. "John and Sue Harris; he sat at their table uninvited." A third finger. "He ruined Steven's card trick." A fourth.

"Card trick?"

"Steven is a magician."

Kingery stared at her.

"Well, he is," Christine said. "It's a hobby, I guess, but he also does it for money. He's really good."

"Was Mr. Kutcher angry when Mr. Cornell spoiled his … magic trick?" Kingery asked with a disdainful smirk and a lift of one eyebrow.

So much for Christine's theory that his facial muscles were somehow paralyzed. "Angry?" she said. "That's a big word. *Peeved*, I'd say, maybe. Irritated."

"Not irritated enough to want to kill Mr. Cornell?"

"Of course not. Mr. Cornell was his uncle, anyway."

"Mr. Cornell was Mr. Kutcher's uncle?"

"Well, ex-uncle, I suppose. Janis O'Riordan is Steven's aunt."

Kingery nodded, paused to write in his book.

"Anyone else?"

"Dr. Doherty and his wife. Scott kicked their dog." She

decided not to mention that Lisa had almost gone full Hulk-rage at that incident.

Kingery nodded. "Anyone else?"

"Not that I can think of."

Kingery finished writing in his book, then his eyes lifted to meet Christine's.

"Did you witness a verbal altercation between Mr. Cornell and a" —he checked his notes, then looked back up— "Megan Gravell?"

Shit. She didn't think Mark or Lisa would have mentioned that, so Ronnie must have told him. "Oh yeah, I forgot about that. Scott was rude to her when he was ordering beer. No big deal."

"What was Ms. Gravell's reaction?"

Christine breathed. *May as well be honest. He probably knows anyway.* "She was pretty upset."

"Did you see Ms. Gravell after that incident?"

"Yes, briefly."

"How briefly?" Kingery said.

"I was with her for a minute or so after ... the incident."

"And you didn't see her after that minute or so?"

"No," Christine said, "but I know where she went."

"And where was that?"

"Outside, cooling off. It was my idea."

"Before she went outside," Kingery said, "did she threaten Mr. Cornell in any way?"

"Not that I heard." *Except to say she wanted to kill him.*

Kingery nodded and wrote in his book.

"Ms. Gravell is ... strong, wouldn't you say? For a woman?"

Christine bristled. "What's that supposed to mean?"

"Answer the question."

"I suppose so. I've never arm wrestled her."

"Would you like to?"

Christine gave him the tightest of smiles. "No."

"What time was it when you sent Ms. Gravell out to … *cool off?*"

Uh-oh. "It must have been about five-forty."

"Five-forty. So about the same time Scott Cornell left the taproom."

"I suppose, yes."

"Which happened first?" Kingery said.

"Umm …" Christine temporized, trying to think of a way to avoid answering the question.

"It's a simple question. Did you send Ms. Gravell outside before … or after … Mr. Cornell left the taproom?"

Christine sighed. "Everything happened so fast, it's all blurring together."

Kingery stared at her. He wasn't buying it.

"I'm going to say it was before," she said. She hadn't wanted to draw attention to that particular timeline detail, but Kingery had dragged it out of her anyway.

"So, would you say about five-thirty-five?"

"Maybe. Maybe a couple minutes later."

Kingery wrote that down. "And what time did she come back?"

"After we found the body. Say six-ten, six-fifteen." *Dear God.* This was going south in a hurry.

"Did you see anyone else who had an opportunity to go back to the production area around the same time? They would have had to walk right past you if you were behind the bar, correct?"

"Yes, but I might not necessarily have been looking in that direction. The short answer is no, no one that I … wait a minute." Christine blinked. "Yes. I noticed that Brian Harrison disappeared toward the end of Janis' presentation. And I didn't see him again until after the … after we found the body."

"Did you see him go back the hallway toward the production area?"

"No."

"Could he have gone outside, or elsewhere in the bar?"

"Possibly. Outside was where I eventually found him, after the murder. But I thought it was odd that he chose that time to not be there, when he should have been supporting his wife."

Kingery nodded and gazed at her.

"Also," Christine continued, "Scott's wife Tina, God knows what happened to her. I haven't seen her at all since before the murder. And she was angry with Scott. I don't know what it was about, but you could see it in her face that she was pissed about something."

Kingery wrote in his book. "Let's move on. Do you know the current location of …" —he consulted his notes a couple of pages back— "The transfer pipe? Or bulldog pipe?"

"No. It always hangs on the wall; I'm sure you saw the location. I don't know what happened to it. It was there this morning."

"How can you be sure it was there before the murder?"

"Because …" *Because Megan picked it up and twirled it like Mighty Casey at the bat*, she didn't say. "Because I used it this morning."

"You used it this morning yourself?"

"Yes."

"To do what?" he said.

"To transfer beer from the brite beer tank into a can." A small shading of the truth. She *did* know it had been there this morning, which was the salient point, but she didn't want to tell Kingery the real reason. He was already thinking too much about Megan.

"So when we find it, we might expect to find your fingerprints on it."

"Of course. Mine, Mark's, Kyle's, Megan's. Everyone who works here has touched it at one time or another."

"And who is Kyle?"

"Kyle Waters, one of the owners of Double Groove, and a brewer. He wasn't here today." Christine also had a son named Kyle, but knowing that wasn't the Kyle the detective was asking about, she felt no obligation to volunteer that information.

Kingery nodded, wrote. "The bullpipe is an implement used in the brewing of beer, am I correct?"

"Bulldog pipe. It's really called a transfer pipe. 'Bulldog' refers to its L-shape, like a pipe that you smoke. And yes, it's used in brewing."

"I stand corrected. Since it's a tool used in *brewing*, not *bartending*, would it not be unusual for anyone working *only* as a bartender to touch that pipe?"

"Not ... really." She winced, knowing how lame that had sounded.

"So I might expect to find Ms. Gravell's fingerprints, as well as Mr. Kutcher's and ..." —he paused to check his notes— "Michael Reisinger's?"

Double-shit. He'd caught her.

"I guess it would be unusual to find any of them. But not impossible."

"Understood." He wrote some more notes while Christine fidgeted. "Is there anything else you'd like to tell me?"

Definitely not. "No, not that I can think of."

"Any questions?"

"Actually, yeah, I just thought of something."

He looked up.

"There's a back door to the brewhouse that was

unlocked. *Anybody* could have gotten in that way, and I wouldn't have seen them."

"We're well aware, yes."

"Did you check the security cams outside? There's six of them, two each on two corners of the building, and one on each of the other two corners." Christine had a flare of hope as she realized the cameras could exonerate Megan ... and maybe isolate the real killer, if he or she had entered through the back door. Why hadn't she thought of that sooner?

"We're aware of them as well," Kingery said, "and we're in the process of obtaining that footage. We thought of that all by ourselves."

"Okay, good." Christine exhaled with a sense of relief so palpable that his condescending snarkiness didn't even bother her.

"You're free to go for now, Ms. Buckley," he said without looking at her. "But go back to the taproom, please. I might want to talk to you again."

CHAPTER SEVEN

MEGAN WAS UP next. Christine watched with dismay as her friend went out the door and disappeared. She hadn't had a chance to talk to Megan, tell her what Kingery already knew, what she could still get away with glossing over. And of course, that was more than likely by Kingery's design.

She looked around the taproom and saw that Steven had moved to an empty table across the room, and...

"What happened to Mark and Lisa?" she said.

"While you were in there," Sue Harris said, "Alan told them to go home, but Mark said somebody had to be here to lock up, so he told them to go to their car and wait."

"And he made Steven move over there?" Christine said.

"Yeah. Alan also separated Janis and her husband," Stella said, "and he's watching to make sure nobody uses their phone."

"He's keeping us from talking to each other," Christine said. "So we can't come up with a story."

"What did he ask you?" Stella said.

"Christine," Alan said from the corner of the room, "don't answer that. Do I need to move you to a table by yourself?"

"No," she said. "I get it." She widened her eyes at Stella, who responded with a wince and mouthed *Sorry* to her.

Christine shrugged and waved it off.

The minutes ticked by. Honey, the chocolate Lab, made the rounds of those still present in the taproom, asking for and receiving attention from each person in turn. Meanwhile, a deputy began passing out cups of cold brewery water to anyone who requested one, which was almost everyone. He also set out a bowl for Honey.

Christine tried to sit still, but the longer things dragged on, the more her anxiety got to her. The ability to look at her phone never seemed so essential to everyday life as when it was taken away, and she imagined that by this time, hers were not the only fingers in the taproom itching to play solitaire, or check social media or email, or surf the Net.

She alternated drumming her fingers on the table with bouncing her knee, and for a while, those sufficed to dispel her nervous energy.

"Stop fidgeting," Stella said to her.

"I can't help it," Christine said. "I'm worried about Megan."

Fifteen minutes dragged on to a half hour with still no sign of Megan, and Christine got up and paced.

"Man, they've had her in there a long time," Rick said. "They must really be rakin' her over the coals."

Christine gave him a nasty look. "Don't say that."

"Jeez. Touchy."

By the time Megan had been gone for a full hour, Christine's scalp had broken out in a sweat. "What's taking them so long?" she said.

"I don't know," Rick said, while squinting through the window at the western horizon, where clouds were building, "but I think you mighta been right about one thing. I shoulda left the Chevelle at home."

Christine gasped. "Your car is still here!"

Rick shrugged. "Yeah. Don't seem so important now, though. Considering." A rumble of distant thunder reached them.

"It's coming," John Harris said.

"I wish they'd pick up the pace a little," Stella said, "or else we're all gonna get drenched when we leave here."

Kingery finally finished with Megan, but instead of sending her back to the taproom or to her own car, a deputy marched her out and put her in the back seat of George Booker's Interceptor. They all watched through the window as it happened, mouths agape.

"What's going on now?" Stella asked.

"No idea," Christine said. "But it can't be good." She thought she knew exactly what was going on, but she was afraid to say it aloud.

As the sun set outside, George Booker came into the taproom and talked to Alan Curtis. "We might need to do the people outside next, or let them go home. It's about to storm."

"We'll do the deck people next and then cut 'em loose," Alan said. "Be surprised if any of 'em have much to add, anyway."

Over the next half hour, Kingery beckoned witnesses from the deck to the warehouse next door, one at a time. He spent, on average, about three minutes with each one, and as they came out, they went to their cars and left. Christine saw all three Willig Boys go home, as well as the food truck operators.

Meanwhile, she'd acquired an earworm, courtesy of Mr. Tom Petty, who kept singing in her head that the waiting was the hardest part.

When the deck was finally empty, Kingery invited Jerry McKernan to join him. Jerry was with him for a bit longer than three minutes, and when he eventually did come out, a deputy escorted him along the sidewalk past both of Double Groove's front doors, toward Not Just Vacs.

Next in the barrel was Brian Harrison.

When Brian finished, he came back to the taproom, boxed up his and Janis' belongings from behind the lectern and the table, and carried everything to his car. By the time he'd finished that, Janis, who had followed him to see Kingery, had been dismissed as well. She joined Brian at the car, and they left.

Steven was next. Glancing at the bar clock, Christine saw it was almost nine o'clock. The Sheriff allowed Dr. Doherty to take Honey outside for a brief walk to keep her from consecrating the taproom floor, and they came right back.

After Steven, Kingery called both Dr. Doherty and his wife. They took Honey with them, of course, and they reappeared after around ten minutes had passed, got in their car, and left the premises.

The crowd in the taproom was dwindling. Other than Christine and Megan, everyone who had already talked to Kingery had been sent home, and Christine reflected that this most likely portended ill for one or both of them. Her mind kept coming up with possible explanations, and none of them were particularly appealing to her.

She began to feel the beginnings of a headache.

The rain started, and at almost the same time, Christine felt her phone vibrate once in her pocket. A text had just come in. She turned her head and waited until Alan was looking in another direction, then pulled the phone out of her pocket. She swiveled in her seat so her body would act as a shield while she looked at her phone in her lap. The text was from Ronnie Gaines.

Ronnie: Meet me in the
2nd bathroom, A side.
Dont tell anybody

Christine: WTF pervert

Ronnie: Please. Important

Christine: Now?

Ronnie: Yes

"Christine," Alan said, "are you looking at your phone?"

Feeling herself blush, she turned around and said "Sorry. Just letting my sons know I'm going to be late."

"Put it away."

She nodded, pocketed her phone, and got up from her seat. "Need to hit the ladies' room," she told him. "That okay?"

"Leave your phone on the table," he said.

Wow, she thought. *Alan sure is different when he's in uniform.* But she did understand Alan's reasoning. It must have looked suspicious to him that she'd asked to go to the bathroom right after having been chastised for using her phone. She decided not to hold it against him and placed the phone on the table as she'd been told.

On her way to the bathroom, she considered the wisdom, or lack thereof, of what she was about to do. Ronnie had been known, on several occasions, to make oblique passes at her, and she would ordinarily not allow herself to be caught alone with him. Not that she feared him; she'd simply rather avoid a situation where she had to overtly refuse his advances, which could throw a monkey wrench in their otherwise cordial relationship. But in this case, if what she could discern from reading between the lines of his texts was true – that he needed to talk to her about something having to do with the murder – then it was worth the risk. She needed to hear him out, in case there was something he had to say that might help Megan.

Plus, she had a bone to pick with him.

She passed the first bathroom, paused with her hand on the handle to the second, gathered her courage, and pushed it open. She entered and found Ronnie Gaines leaning against the Roger Dean poster on the opposite wall. "Hey," she said. "What's up?"

"Lock the door."

"Seriously? There's not enough creep factor in meeting me in a bathroom, so you want to ratchet it up by locking the door?"

"Just do it, will you? We can't get caught in here together."

"Oh, man, this is so weird," Christine said, but she did as Ronnie had asked.

"Listen," Ronnie said in a low voice. "They really like Megan for this."

"I guess so," Christine said with a dose of acidity, "since you sold her out."

"I told the truth, that's all."

Up until that moment, she hadn't been entirely certain that it was Ronnie who'd given Megan up. Now she was. "She didn't do it," she said.

"Then she's got nothing to worry about. The truth will come out."

Christine snorted. "Are you really that naïve?"

Ronnie sighed. "Look, can we … I didn't ask you in here to fight with me. I'm trying to help."

Christine took a moment to settle herself down. "Fine. Let's start over. What've you got?"

"Thanks," Ronnie said, having the grace to look

abashed. "So, it's bad. They think Cornell was lured back there by a phone call or a text, but they can't find his phone to prove it. The M.E. got here, and he says Scott was killed by a blow to the back of the neck, and it was somebody strong that did it. They won't know for sure until the autopsy, but it looks like it was what they call 'internal decapitation.' Severed the spinal cord. Dead before he hit the floor."

"That's why there wasn't much blood."

"Yeah," Ronnie said. "His nose broke, and it gushed blood for a few seconds, but that's it."

"What about the cameras?"

"They aren't working. They're controlled by a computer next door, in the back room of Not Just Vacs. A deputy took Jerry over there to show him, but when they got there they found out the cameras were all down."

"What do you mean, *down*?" Christine said. "All of them? At the same time?"

"Yeah. Remember that thunderstorm two weeks ago?"

Christine nodded. "How could I forget? It was scary as hell."

"The building took a strike," Ronnie said. "The siding is steel and it's continuous all the way around the building, so when lightning hit it, it fried the circuit boards in all the cameras at the same time."

"And nobody knew it until now?"

"Jerry's son handles all that, and he's been on vacation. Jerry and the other employees never look at the feed unless something happens, and nothing ever happens around here."

Christine shook her head in disgust. "That's just marvelous."

"It gets worse. They might have struck out on the cameras, but guess what they *did* find at Not Just Vacs."

Christine shrugged. "Just tell me." She was trying to behave, but she was still irritated with him.

"The transfer pipe. Under a table in the back, behind some old sewing machines. With some hair and blood on it. Don't know *whose* hair and blood for now, but what would be your guess?"

Christine's jaw dropped. "How did it get there?"

Ronnie nodded. "That's the right question. The killer couldn't have gone through the front door. They would have had to walk through a crowd of people carrying a bloody stainless steel pipe. But they could have gone out the *back* door of Double Groove and in the back door of Not Just Vacs without being seen. The problem is that, unlike Double Groove, Not Just Vacs was closed, and the back door was locked. And that means whoever stashed the murder weapon in there had to have a key to Not Just Vacs' back door."

Christine's heart thudded in her chest. Only two people in the brewpub tonight would have had that key. Jerry McKernan, the building's owner, was one.

The other was Megan, who worked part-time at Not Just Vacs.

"Oh my God," she said.

Ronnie nodded. "Didn't take you long."

"I can understand why ... I mean, it looks bad, I get it."

"So, earlier you said she didn't do it. Are you sure, a hundred percent sure?"

"Yes!" *No?*

"Because if they find Megan's prints on that thing, it's all over. Are they gonna find her prints on it?"

Christine tipped her head back and looked at the ceiling as she sighed.

"I guess I can take that as a yes?" Ronnie said.

"I should have told Kingery earlier, but I was trying not

to make Megan seem dangerous. This morning, we had a tennis ball in the brewhouse, and Megan picked up the pipe and held it like she was in the batter's box waiting for a pitch."

"She's toast," Ronnie said, shaking his head. "I shouldn't be telling you any of this, but I know you two are close. What makes you think she's innocent? If you have anything that can prove she's in the clear, now's the time to bring it up."

"I talked to her by FaceTime," she said. "I could see she was in her car."

"Okay. That's good. What time?"

"Right after we discovered the body."

"That doesn't help," Ronnie said. "We need to know where she was at the time of the murder, not after it."

"But I could tell by her reaction when I told her about it. Megan's a lot of things, but a good actor isn't one of them. She was legit surprised when I told her." *And tickled pink.*

"But you can't prove it."

"No," she said, "I guess not. It was FaceTime. I don't think you can save it, and even if you can, I didn't. It's gone."

"Listen, you're biased and they know it. I don't think *your* memory of how *you* read her reaction through a phone screen is gonna be enough to outweigh the physical evidence."

"What about her phone? You have that?"

"Yeah," Ronnie said.

"If she texted Scott, it would be on her phone," she said in triumph.

"Unless she deleted it."

"You can't find out from the provider if she did that?"

"We can, but it takes seven to ten days to get that info."

Deflated, Christine closed her eyes and growled in

frustration. Seven to ten days in jail would reduce Megan to a gibbering idiot. There had to be another way out of this dilemma. "She's not the only one that disappeared around the time of the murder, you know."

"I know, and those other people aren't completely in the clear yet. But right now, Kingery is focused on Megan, and when he gets like that, he's like a dog that won't drop the ball. If I'm honest, I kind of don't blame him this time. She looks like a slam-dunk to me."

"Damn it, Ronnie. You *know* Megan. You know she's not a killer."

"I'm not the one that needs to be convinced."

A clever answer, and one that Christine noticed did not confirm or deny her last statement. "So why am I still here?" she said. "Everybody else got released after they were questioned."

"Kingery thought you were lying to him. He wanted a chance to talk to you again later. And he was right, wasn't he?"

"Not really. I mean, I didn't lie about anything that matters. Oh my God, am I a suspect?"

"I don't know. Did you kill him?"

"Of course not!"

"Yeah, I know you didn't," Ronnie said. "But you lied by omission, at the least. You didn't tell him about Megan touching the pipe this morning. Which was a mistake, if you're trying to do right by Megan. It would have established an explanation for her fingerprints being on it, but now it's too late. If you change your story now, it'll look like you made it up."

"Yeah. I see that now. I should have told him, but the questions were coming so fast, I didn't have time to think. I got confused, and I screwed up."

"That's what happens when you start lying." Ronnie

shook his head. "Word of advice: if he takes you back in there, come clean. He doesn't take kindly to evasiveness. But anyway, I don't even know if that's on the table anymore, now that he thinks he's got his killer."

"This is insane."

"I know it's hard for you, and I'm sorry. I just wanted to give you a heads up about what was coming, in case you knew anything that could get her off. But I gotta get back outside. Wait a couple minutes after I leave before you go. And don't tell anybody about our conversation."

Christine nodded. "Thanks," she said, coming as close as she could to offering an olive branch.

Ronnie nodded back and slipped out and into the brewhouse. She locked the door behind him. She figured she may as well use the hardware while she was there, so she did that and then went back to her table.

"Is Steven still over there with Kingery?" she asked as she slid back onto her stool.

"No," Rick said. "They just let him go."

They waited to find out who was next. But after Steven, Kingery failed to show up to ask for another witness. Instead, the same deputy who had earlier escorted Jerry to Not Just Vacs now entered the taproom from the brewhouse. He walked straight through the taproom and out the front door to Booker's car. He took Megan out of the car, holding his Stetson over her to protect her from the rain, and escorted *her* back to Kingery's "office."

A second interview, in this case, was not something anyone yearned for.

Christine's nerves were getting the best of her. She did some more finger drumming. Her headache, surely a manifestation of the unrelenting tension, had now assumed colossal proportions.

In less than five minutes, she received another text.

Christine stole a glance at her phone, which was still lying on the table where Alan had told her to put it before she went to the bathroom, and saw it was Ronnie again.

"Stella," she said, "do you have any ibuprofen or anything? My head's killing me."

"I think so," Stella said, and fumbled around in her purse until she produced a bottle. She passed it across the table to Christine.

As Christine took the bottle and pulled it back toward herself, she used the motion to surreptitiously slide her phone back into her lap. "Thanks," she said. She popped the bottle and swallowed two ibuprofen, then passed it back to Stella.

"Actually," Stella said as she took the bottle back, "I think I could use a couple, too."

Christine turned her chair as she'd done earlier. Alan either hadn't noticed her maneuver or didn't care anymore. She opened her phone's lock screen and read the text.

> **Ronnie:** They charged her
> they have her out back in
> cuffs shes going to jail

>> **Christine:** Can't you vouch for her?

> **Ronnie:** Probable cause,
> out of my hands

>> **Christine:** {anger emoji}

Then, through the window, Christine caught sight of another Sheriff's Office Interceptor coming from behind the building. She watched as it exited the parking lot and turned left onto Robin Circle.

With Megan inside.

CHAPTER EIGHT

WITH ALL THE key witnesses having been interviewed, Kingery now started working through the remaining people in the taproom. Looking around the room, Christine counted fewer than ten people still waiting to be released. The Rineers went first, although it was too late to prevent the Chevelle from getting rained on. The rest went relatively quickly, but not quickly enough for Christine's headache, not to mention her back and butt, both of which were growing sore from sitting on her hard metal stool for so long.

As Christine waited, wondering if she was going to get the dreaded second interview, she realized that, besides Tina Cornell, another person was missing, one she'd forgotten about until just this moment.

Keith Bonham. She hadn't seen him since before the book reading began.

She felt a twisting in her gut as she made a connection that hadn't occurred to her until this very moment. Recalling the moment when she'd first seen Scott's body and thought for a brief second that it was Mark's, she mentally compared the two men's size and build. Also the short salt-and-pepper hair that they both shared, as well as the fact that Scott's hat covered his distinguishing bald spot. Christine grew excited as suspicion bloomed and a new scenario took form in her mind.

What if whoever had killed Scott had come to the brewhouse looking not for Scott, but for Mark? What if they had then seen Scott from behind, exactly where they'd naturally expect to find Mark, assumed it *was* Mark, and struck to kill?

Combined with the knowledge that Keith Bonham had lingered in the area after his confrontation with Mark, this new revelation convinced Christine that she'd figured the whole thing out.

Keith Bonham was the culprit.

But it was only a theory at this point. To put the final nail in this coffin, she'd need to establish Bonham's whereabouts at the time of the murder. She cast her mind back. The last time she remembered seeing him had been right after the arrival of the O'Riordan party, walking toward the food truck. She hadn't seen him since, but that didn't mean he hadn't still been there at the time of the murder. Christine simply hadn't been paying much attention to what was going on outside the taproom. With the damned cameras down, how could she find out what had happened to Keith Bonham after that last sighting? Had he, by any chance, slipped behind the building after that?

The logical first step would be to ask the guys in the food truck. If Bonham, or anybody else, had walked around to the back of the building, they would have crossed right in front of the food truck, and they'd have been visible through the truck's windshield for the entire walk along the side of the building. The guys working in the truck would've seen him … if they happened to be looking in that direction.

The food truck had already packed up and left, but she could find them. It was as simple as checking their website for the schedule. And she would do exactly that, and she would find them. Hopefully tomorrow, if they weren't too far out of the area.

The next half-hour or so, as Kingery talked to everyone that was left, was anticlimactic. Adding to her discomfort, Christine now felt a growling in her stomach, and cursed her own stupidity in not ever having made it to the food truck herself before they left, but at least the hunger pangs helped to keep her awake. With nowhere to go, nothing to do but wait, nothing to eat, and nothing to drink other than brewery water, the few still in the taproom grew bored and increasingly irritable as the minutes wore on. Christine figured she wasn't the only one suffering from a sore back, butt, belly, or head. Although she might be the only one suffering from all four at the same time.

She found herself humming "The Waiting" again. *Damn that song.*

The clock showed five minutes short of ten o'clock when the last man went to see Kingery, leaving only Alan Curtis and Christine in the taproom. A few minutes later the man drove away, and Christine looked at Alan with an inquisitive lift of her brow. Alan said nothing.

Kingery came through the taproom door. "You can go," he said to Christine. "But don't leave town for the next few days, until we get this sorted out."

Christine was irritated, and she couldn't stop herself. "You couldn't have said that an hour and a half ago?"

"Sorry for your inconvenience," he said. Then he and Alan Curtis went back to the brewhouse, leaving Christine alone in the room.

She rose and went to the door, where she stopped.

Outside the door, it was raining axe handles and pitchforks, and she had parked her vehicle behind Double Groove. She assumed she still wasn't allowed to go through the brewhouse, and she had no umbrella, no hat, nothing.

Resigned to her fate, she pushed through the door and trudged in the rain all the way around the building. By the time she got to her vehicle, her hair and shirt were soaked, she couldn't see through her glasses, and her feet were swimming in her shoes. One final indignity added to the end of a day-long debacle.

After starting the engine and flipping the wipers on, she noticed the silhouettes of two heads in the front seat of the car parked in front of her. Mark and Lisa, still waiting for everyone to leave so they could lock up. She called them and updated them about what had gone on after they'd been sent out. Mark listened, then said, "Don't worry about Megan. I've got a lawyer for her, and I'm gonna call him first thing in the morning. He's expensive, but he's the best, and we'll help her pay for it. Maybe we'll have a benefit."

Christine nodded, then realized he couldn't see her nodding her head, and said, "That sounds good. Thanks."

"Go home and try to get some sleep."

Christine scoffed. "Fat chance. But I'll try. You do the same."

She made it home purely on autopilot, her mind lost in a semi-daze. Muscle memory delivered her to her driveway, and as she pulled into it, it occurred to her that she had no recollection of the drive between Double Groove and the stop sign at the entrance to her street. She climbed out of her car, slammed the door behind her, scampered through the rain to her front door, and finally stumbled, dripping wet, body-sore, and emotionally drained, into her home.

Bobby was there to meet her, and if he'd been dressed as Lady Gaga, Christine wouldn't have noticed. She only wanted his warmth and his love, and as he wrapped her in his arms, no words were exchanged and none were needed. She sagged into him and let the day drain away.

* * *

"Did you get anything to eat?" Bobby asked later, after she'd changed into dry clothing.

"No. Kept thinking about going to the food truck, but I never did, and then the fit hit the Shan, and it was too late."

"Got spaghetti here. And a microwave."

"That'll do."

Christine gave Bobby the rundown between shoveled mouthfuls of spaghetti.

"Megan?" Bobby said. "No way."

"Right? That's what I'm saying. If you could've seen her face when I told her about the murder. You know how she is."

"Heart's on her sleeve at all times."

"Exactly. No way she was pretending. She was honest-to-God surprised. I'd bet the Shelby on it."

"Does she have a lawyer?"

"Mark's got a guy for her. Says he's the best. He's calling him in the morning."

Bobby lifted an eyebrow. "Mark just happens to know the best defense lawyer in town?"

"He's a Mason, remember? He has all sorts of connections."

"Oh, yeah," Bobby said. "Well, cool. There's nothing to worry about, then."

"Are you kidding? So much could still go wrong. They'll have her prints on the murder weapon, they have witnesses that'll talk about how mad she was, and they have the fact that nobody knew where she was when it happened.

Means, motive, and opportunity. And I don't care how good of a lawyer you have, you never know what twelve random people are gonna say."

Bobby sighed. "I wish there was a way to help."

Christine finished chewing. Then she swallowed and turned slowly to face Bobby and stared at him.

"Oh, no," Bobby said. "What are you thinkin' about?"

"There is a way. I'm gonna figure out who really did it and I'm gonna prove it. I already have an idea where to start."

"Christine. That's why we have police."

Christine shook her head. "That guy, that detective, Kingery, he's got his mind made up. He's not going to look at all the facts. He's got a prime suspect and he's going to stick with her."

"You don't know—"

"Not for a fact, no. But I got a strong vibe from him, and Ronnie more or less corroborated it for me … No, I'm not leaving this up to chance. And that guy."

"What do you think you can do?"

"For starters," Christine said as she got up from the table, "Facebook."

"How can that help?"

"That platform was practically built for stalking. I'll just poke around, learn about Scott's friends, maybe find some trolls. Just to get some ideas." She rinsed her plate off and put it in the dishwasher. "Where's my phone?"

"Right here."

Christine sat back at the table and picked up her phone.

A few minutes later, she gave up without having learned much. Scott Cornell's profile was private. His wife didn't have one that Christine could find. She checked LinkedIn, Instagram, Snapchat, and that platform that she still referred to as Twitter, refusing to use its moronic new name.

Nada. The woman was an online ghost. Christine figured she may have had accounts under another name. Or ... maybe she had deleted all her accounts since earlier today ... a possibility that had hair-raising implications, but one Christine didn't have the wherewithal to pursue at the moment.

Instead, she went to Janis O'Riordan's Facebook page, thinking she might find something there, but it was predictably focused on her writing career, not her relatives or friends or any drama that might accompany them.

She did find one thing, not very promising, but it was a thread she could tug on. It was a post from a Facebook group dedicated to fans of Janis O'Riordan. Fan groups like that knew all the dirt. That dirt might even extend to their idol's ex-husband's dirt. It was a long shot, but what the hell? A long shot was better than no shot.

The group was private and based in Bel Air, Maryland. She joined it and messaged the administrator, someone named Shane Ritchie.

Maybe she'd have a reply by morning. Maybe this guy knew something and would be willing to help her out.

Maybe, maybe, maybe ...

But in all the murder mysteries she'd ever read, that was the way the investigators did it. Just keep throwing stuff at the wall, and see what sticks.

"I'm gonna hit the hay," Bobby said. "You still wanna go to Elkton in the morning to see that truck, or are you too burned out?"

"I still want to go. I'm coming to bed too. Can't throw anything else at the wall tonight, anyway."

"Huh?"

"Never mind."

CHAPTER NINE

THE NEXT MORNING, Bobby and Christine got up early, dressed, and rousted the boys. Christine tested her ankle and found the injury was but a shadow of what it had been.

They had a quick breakfast, and the four of them gathered what few belongings they needed for the hour's drive to Elkton, Maryland.

Outside, as the family loaded themselves into the Highlander with Bobby taking the wheel, the skies were blue and cloudless, and the air fairly throbbed with the whirring calls of morning cicadas in the trees.

Minutes into their journey, the Highlander's air conditioning had banished both the warmth and the humidity. There was little traffic, and the scenery was bucolic and pleasant. Bobby hummed along with the radio, while Evan and Kyle bickered in the back seat, but Christine barely heard any of it. Her mind was on Megan, wondering how her friend was feeling after her night in jail.

Uncomfortable, alone, and scared, most likely.

It was intolerable.

She called Mark.

"I contacted my friend the defense attorney," he said. "He's gonna get Megan out today, if at all possible. If he can't do it, nobody can."

"Wow, that's a big relief," Christine said. "I guess the bill's mounting up already, huh?"

"I had to pay a deposit."

"Out of your pocket?"

"Yeah. No big deal. But I'm afraid I have news you're not gonna like."

Christine braced herself. "What's that?"

"We both know Megan didn't do it, but I can't let her work at Double Groove while she's the number one suspect. It's an optics thing."

Christine sighed. "I understand. Can you pay her, at least?"

"Of course. Same thing at Not Just Vacs, so she's on indefinite leave from both places until this gets cleared up."

"Which it will. I'll do it myself, if I have to."

They hung up.

Christine had to figure out who the real killer was, and soon.

As they crossed the Susquehanna on Conowingo Dam, she watched the bald eagles soaring against the backdrop of the trees on the opposite bank, and she began to think about her own list of suspects.

Number One: Megan. Eliminated. Move on.

Number Two, and Christine's current favorite: Keith Bonham, who, in her scenario, was so angry with Mark that he snuck in the rear entrance, saw Scott Cornell from the rear, thought it was Mark, and killed him, then dragged the body around the corner, and used the back door again for his escape. Maybe he'd become aware of his mistake by then, maybe not. It didn't matter.

One problem with that scenario: How did he get the

murder weapon into the rear of Not Just Vacs? She made a mental note to seek out Jerry McKernan later today, and ask him if the back door to his store was always kept locked. The cops had most likely asked the same question, but since Christine had no way of knowing what the cops might had overlooked, she was going on the premise that she needed to verify everything, down to the simplest and most routine of inquiries. If she assumed a question had been asked, when in fact it hadn't, her entire investigation would be flawed.

On to Suspects Number Three and Three-Point-Five: keeping an open mind, could Mark and/or Lisa have been so righteously pissed at Scott that one of them did the deed themselves? Lisa, in particular, had been present when Scott kicked the dog, and Christine had witnessed her reaction. Christine also remembered that Scott had once been fired for stealing beer recipes, something that, if Mark knew about it, would not endear Scott to him, should he find the man trespassing in Double Groove's brewhouse without an escort.

But no. Christine had seen both Moodys in moods before, but she knew them well enough to know that murder was not in their blood, no matter how livid they might get. Moreover, Lisa was probably not tall enough or strong enough to have accomplished the deed unaided.

And again, there was the question of the back door to Not Just Vacs. That problem was going to keep coming up with respect to any potential killer Christine looked into, outside of Jerry and Megan, and it was one she'd need to solve quickly. Because if she couldn't, she might as well give up now.

At any rate, she had already eliminated Mark and Lisa as suspects in her own mind, but she had no objective evidence for it, so she kept them on her list for that reason only.

She opened a new Note on her phone and started typing in the high points of her thought processes regarding each suspect. After catching up with Suspects One, Two, Three, and Three-Point-Five, she moved on.

Number Four: Brian Harrison. As Janis O'Riordan's current husband, was it possible there was still bad blood between him and her ex-husband, Scott Cornell? Maybe even a bit of lingering jealousy? Christine had witnessed tension between Brian and Janis after Scott had made his big entrance, going directly to Janis to wrap her in a bear hug and call her "baby." Brian also had disappeared around the time of the murder, which gave him opportunity as well as motive. He couldn't be ruled out.

Number Five: Janis O'Riordan herself. Unlikely. Yes, she had been visibly repulsed when Scott hugged her, and she'd shown signs of embarrassment, maybe even anger, when he acted up during her reading. But she had a pretty solid alibi. She'd been standing in the taproom in front of fifty other people during the entire time Scott had been absent. Eliminated.

Number Six: Scott's wife, Tina Cornell. Christine had seen the two of them quarreling as well. Tina had vanished sometime before the murder, and Christine hadn't seen her since. But Tina was another, like Lisa, who didn't look the part, physically speaking. While average in height, she was thin and had been wearing a tight dress and heels. Not the sort of garb that lent itself to the swinging of a long pipe with enough force to kill someone. It seemed doubtful to Christine, but she would ask around about that one, and see if she could find a witness to her whereabouts at the crucial time.

Number Seven: Jerry McKernan. As the other person who had access to the back room of Not Just Vacs, where the murder weapon had been found, he had to be considered. Christine knew for a fact that he'd been at the party, but she hadn't paid attention to his location during any of it, let alone the slice of time in question. And what would his motive have been? She didn't think he'd even known who Scott Cornell was before yesterday, and if he had, that had yet to come out. The only thing Christine could think of, and it was a reach, was that maybe Jerry had seen how Scott treated Megan, whom he indulged like a daughter, and he'd snapped and killed Scott in a fit of protective rage.

Didn't seem likely.

And last, Number Eight: Represented by a simple question mark in Christine's notes, this was a hypothetical unknown person who had an unknown beef with Scott Cornell. Judging by what she knew of Scott's character, that list might be long, but until she found a way to dig into his past, she couldn't put a name or a face to this nebulous suspect. The taproom had been full of people yesterday, a good portion of whom Christine had never seen before. Any one of them could have been that person from Scott's past that was nursing a grudge serious enough to culminate in murder.

"You okay?" Bobby asked.

They'd been together long enough that short silences between them had ceased to be uncomfortable years ago. But silence that stretched from Conowingo to the north side of Rising Sun, as this one had, was atypical and usually meant one of them was mad, or both.

"Yeah," she said, "sorry. Just thinking about …"

"Megan."

"Yeah."

Bobby nodded. "Okay. As long it's not something I said."

"No, it's not you." She reached across the center console and patted his thigh in reassurance. "Definitely not you."

Christine became aware that the kids had grown quiet as well. Twelve-year-old Kyle had headphones on his ears and his nose in a comic book; and Evan, two years younger, had his phone in his right hand while miming guitar chords with his left, as he watched guitar lessons on YouTube. She'd never seen a child so young get so immersed in learning how to play guitar. She hoped he'd stick with it.

She looked out the window and lapsed back into thought. Another idea had occurred to her. This Shane Ritchie guy, the administrator of Janis' fan club on Facebook, had probably been at the event last night, and she bet he'd taken some pictures. Now that she'd joined the group, she could check its page again and see if he'd posted any. If he hadn't, she could ask him to share any he might have with her. Some of these might turn out to be useful as visual evidence, to establish the locations of some of her suspects at the time of the murder.

As she finished that thought, her phone dinged. She checked and found that she'd received a Facebook message from Shane.

Wow, she thought. *Speak of the devil.*

In the message, he indicated he'd be happy to speak with her, gave her his personal phone number, and said he'd be available for a call after two o'clock today.

Cool. Smiling to herself, she added that to her mental list for later. Things were shaking. This Jessica Fletcher gig was not without its psychic rewards.

Then, hoping there was no lingering tension between her and Ronnie Gaines, she somewhat shamelessly exploited their relationship and texted him as well, asking in broad terms how the investigation was going.

He texted her back.

Ronnie: Meet me at DG at 3?

She smiled. This meant two things. First, he'd brushed off their little snit last night, as she had. Second, the fact that he didn't want to put something in a text must mean he wanted it to be off the record. And that could be good news or bad news, but either way, it could only help her in her mission.

Christine: Sure

Ronnie: {Thumbs-up emoji}

The to-do list was up to several items now, so she started another Note.

TO DO
Food truck
Jerry/back door locked?
Check pics/Facebook
Call Shane
Ronnie

Two of them she could work on right now.

She checked the website of yesterday's food truck, and found that ... *Hah!* ... it would be at Double Groove again today. That was more convenience than she had any right to expect. She would talk to the operators when she got there, and find out if any of them had noticed Keith Bonham going behind the building yesterday.

Next, she went to the Janis O'Riordan Fan Group's Facebook page and checked for pictures from last night's event. There were none, nor was there any mention of the book release party other than a posting from a week ago that announced the event and established its time and venue.

Maybe some pics would show up later, maybe not. Maybe Shane Ritchie had simply deemed it in poor taste to post pics of an event at which a murder had occurred, which would be understandable. She left it on her list, along with the food truck.

"Are you gonna put that phone down before we get there?" Bobby asked, breaking into her thought processes again.

"Sorry," she said, dropping the phone in her lap. "I'm done."

"Good. 'Cause we're two minutes away."

CHAPTER TEN

CHRISTINE STARTED TO feel uneasy as soon as they pulled into the long dirt driveway with the tumble-down farmhouse at the end of it.

"Are you sure this is the right place?" she asked.

"According to the GPS," Bobby said, pointing to the display on the dash. "We're looking for 214 Redman Road, right?"

Christine checked the listing on her phone. "Yeah, that's right."

"Well, here we are."

"Where? Bigfoot County?"

They approached the house at a turtle's pace as Bobby slalomed around potholes of unknown depth, still filled to the brim with muddy water from the rains last night. Christine saw a frog jump into one as they neared it, the resulting disturbance causing a cloud of gnats and mosquitos to erupt from its surface. Parked near the house were an old Dodge Ram pickup and a decrepit-looking Kia sedan. Neither vehicle had been washed in years, by the looks of them.

"There's no garage," Christine said.

"Noticed that," Bobby said.

"This can't be right."

A potbellied man in cutoff jeans and a greasy John Deere trucker hat stepped out of the house's front door and onto the porch, letting the screen door slam behind him with a crack that they heard through the closed windows of the Highlander. As he walked down the three sagging wooden steps to ground level, he took a final drag off his cigarette and flicked it into the ratty grass near the cracked concrete sidewalk, where it joined a hundreds-strong colony of similar dead soldiers.

"Is it just me, or are you getting *Deliverance* vibes, too?" Christine said.

Bobby snickered. "Chill out, it ain't that bad." He lowered his window. "You Frank?" he said to the guy in cutoffs.

"That's me," the man said.

Bobby parked, and the four of them climbed out and walked to meet Frank. After introductions all around, Bobby said, "So where you keepin' the truck?"

"Oh, it's around back in the shed. Snug as a bug in a rug. Wanna see it? Follow me."

As they walked around the house, Christine's sense of dismay grew and grew. A foul odor trailed behind Frank, a rancid cocktail of sweat, cigarettes, cat urine, and mildew that almost triggered Christine's gag reflex. An old white refrigerator stood in the yard, its doors open to the elements. The side yard was composed almost entirely of crabgrass, the tasseled seedstalks of which tickled Christine's ankles as they walked through it. Passing an open window on the house, she heard an oscillating fan whirring inside, and as threadbare curtains fluttered out the window, more of that rancid cocktail wafted out.

Christine couldn't get "Dueling Banjos" out of her head. She caught Bobby's eye. With no words exchanged, she knew he was thinking the same thing she was. Something was really wrong here.

"So once upon a time," Frank said, "the truck belonged to my grandpa. When he died … he raised me, y'know, my folks both died when I was real little … anyway, when he died, it came down to me. Now I ain't never driven it, to tell ya the truth, but Gramps, he took real good care of it. In fact, he spent so much time on it, I think that's why Grandma left him."

Frank turned and gave Bobby a gap-toothed grin to show that this was a joke, or at least truth-in-jest, so Bobby and Christine gave polite chuckles in response.

Then the shed came into view, and Christine lost any hope that this truck might be a good find, even for the absurdly low price at which it had been listed.

It was large for a shed, almost barn-sized, but it was sided with wooden planks that had gone grey with age and shrunk so that numerous gaps appeared between them. Portions of some planks had rotted or broken and fallen off completely. The roof was of slate shingles, some of which hung askew, and all of which sported a colony of bright green moss. There were two windows visible, both of them multi-pane, and neither had all the panes intact.

Frank walked up to the sliding barn door and shoved it to his left. Or tried to. The barn door refused to move.

"Hm," he said. "Must be rusty."

"There's a bunch of rocks and dirt piled here," Bobby said, "where the door's supposed to go to."

"Oh yeah," Frank said. "Forgot I dropped that bucketload there. Hafta move it."

"Hasn't anyone else been here to look at it yet?" Christine said.

"Nope. You're the first," Frank said as he lifted a head-size rock and tossed it aside. "Couple pulled into the driveway but turned around and left."

"How long's the truck been in here?"

"Let's see," Frank said. "Grandpa died six years ago, so at least that long."

"When was that picture taken, the one you have online?"

"Before that."

As Frank continued to move rocks away from the barn door, Christine and Bobby exchanged another look.

Frank moved the last rock, and this time when he pushed on the door, it ground and stuttered its way open.

Frank, Bobby, and Christine stepped inside the shed. If the exterior looked dilapidated, the inside was far worse. "Stay out there, boys," Bobby said. "It's not safe."

They found the truck sunk to the axles in mud.

"You've got a raccoon or something living in the cab," Christine said, thinking, *I'd hate to see what's under the hood.*

Clear evidence of body cancer showed itself around the wheel wells and running boards, and the truck's hood had been adorned with a wide stripe of pigeon droppings, directly under the line of an overhead hand-hewn wooden beam.

The price, which had seemed almost too good to be true, turned out to be far too high for a truck in this condition.

"This is too much of a project for us," Bobby said, turning away.

"Aw, come on," Frank said. "Just needs a little work, that's all. I'll cut you a break on the price."

"Frank," Bobby said, pulling no punches, "we were looking for something more or less road-ready, and that's what you advertised, but this ain't it. You just wasted two hours of our time. I wish you luck."

* * *

On the way back, between Megan being in jail and the truck being a total dead end, Christine found herself spiraling into a black mood. She stared out the window for a while, making obligatory responses to Bobby's attempts to cheer her up, until she caught hold of the lip of whatever pit she was falling into and hauled herself back up.

Oh well, she thought. *On to the next truck.*

And back to the murder investigation.

By eleven o'clock that morning, she and the boys were back at home. Before entering the house, they all checked each other for ticks. Then Christine left Bobby with the boys and returned to Double Groove for her afternoon shift.

In the brewhouse, she found Mark, black-bearded Kyle, and instead of the usual bready aroma, the overpowering smells of bleach and disinfectant.

"I'm out of here," Mark said, as he dug a fist into the small of his back and rolled his neck, exhaustion etched into the lines of his face. "I was here until three in the morning cleaning up, and right back again at eight. But we're good to go. At least there wasn't much blood. I hate to think what it would've been like if he'd been shot."

"Go on, get out of here," Kyle said. "Get some sleep. We got this." Then, seeming to remember Christine had been through the mill as well, he turned to her and said, "You okay, Chris?"

"Yeah," she said. "I'm good. But how we going to can this Gimme Three Hops without a transfer pipe? The cops took ours, right?"

"Gotcha covered," Mark said, picking up a pipe from the desk. "Borrowed this from Slate." The local community of breweries, though business rivals, looked out for each other in time of need.

Kyle had already gotten the whole story from Mark, so

there was no need for Christine to bring him up to speed. They got straight to work transferring the new Gimme Three Hops from the brite tank to kegs and cans. They did a single keg first, to slough off the majority of the particles. Then they did a batch of sixteen-ounce cans to be sold in the case out front, and then filled seven more kegs, leaving the brite tank empty.

When they were finished, as Kyle cleaned up, Christine walked next door to Not Just Vacs, which was open by that time. She pushed open the door, triggering the bells to jingle, and by the time she reached the counter, Jerry McKernan, tall and grey, had emerged from the office to join her on the other side of the counter.

He looked almost as bad as Mark had.

"Hey, Christine," he said.

"Hi, Jerry. Rough night, huh?"

"You could say that."

"You holding up okay?"

"As well as can be expected," he said, "considering. I just can't believe she'd do something like that."

"What if she didn't?"

Jerry stared at her. "What do you mean? She obviously did."

"It's not obvious to me. I spoke to her right after the murder, and I told her about it. I could tell she was surprised. In fact, she was kind of happy the guy was dead, which isn't something a guilty person would ordinarily say."

Christine had to be careful here. She knew there was still a remote possibility that Jerry himself had done the deed, for some reason unknown. Maybe to protect Megan, after he'd seen Scott be so rude to her. Seemed like a flimsy motive, but she didn't really know Jerry that well, and sometimes people had demons you couldn't see.

At any rate, she didn't want to give too much away to

someone who might benefit from Megan taking the fall. She'd rather he went right along thinking no one was on to him, and maybe make a mistake out of complacency.

"I guess that's true," he said with a trace of peevishness. "But someone got into that back door, and if it wasn't her, it had to be me. And it wasn't me."

Her witness was getting defensive with her already, and she hadn't even asked a question. But there was one question she needed answered, and only Jerry could answer it.

"Listen," she said. "I know it's not my place to ask, but just to satisfy my curiosity, that door was definitely locked?"

"Yes, of course. I told the police that last night."

Christine nodded. "Would you mind if I looked at it? I'm just searching for some other explanation, anything that doesn't point directly at Megan."

Jerry's mouth was set in a straight line. "Christine—"

"Think about Megan. Imagine just for a second that she's innocent, sitting in jail, suffering, knowing she's going to get pinched for something she didn't do. She's family to both of us. Isn't it worth double-checking, if there's a chance we could get her out of there?"

Jerry sighed. "Come on," he said. Smiling, she stepped behind the counter and followed him into the back room, past tables loaded with disassembled vacuum cleaners and sewing machines. "That's Megan's station, where they found the pipe," Jerry said, pointing.

They zigzagged their way past all the tables to the rear entrance. "This is the door," he said, the motion of his hand giving her tacit permission to do as she would. "They fingerprinted the doorknob, of course."

"And?"

"Mine, my wife's, my son's, and Megan's."

"Naturally."

It was a standard thirty-six-inch hollow steel door with no windows, knob on the right, opening outward. A hydraulic door closer was mounted to the top of it. Fine black fingerprint dust coated the door surface around the knob, but the knob itself had been wiped clean since last night. No deadbolt. Christine grasped the knob and alternately pushed and pulled on the door without turning the knob. There was some give in the fit. "Get a lot of cold air through there in the wintertime?" she asked.

"You better believe it."

Then she turned the knob, opened the door, and stepped outside. "I'm gonna let it shut," she said. "Don't leave me out here."

Jerry nodded.

The door swung closed, and she heard the latch strike home. She grasped the knob and tried to turn it. No dice. It was locked. She shook the door as she had from the inside. She gave it a couple of good solid yanks, and the latch held. It had some play in it, as she'd already established from the inside, but the door was solidly closed.

She examined the doorframe around the striker plate. There was some sloppiness there as well, a gap of almost a quarter of an inch between the door and the striker plate. She pulled her debit card from her pants pocket and inserted it into the slot, angled it a bit to get behind the latch, and pulled it back toward herself. The latch slid neatly back, and the door opened.

Jerry stood on the other side, mouth agape.

"Now, I admit," Christine said, "that I'm handy with tools and mechanical stuff. But if I could do it that easily …"

"Anyone could."

Christine only nodded. "You might want to look into a

deadbolt."

CHAPTER ELEVEN

ON HER WAY back to Double Groove, Christine could barely contain herself. She'd just eliminated the one major roadblock to her finding an alternative explanation for Scott Cornell's murder.

She also was able to definitively eliminate the lingering doubts she had about whether Jerry could have been complicit, perhaps propping the door open for the killer, or something of that nature. But between the fact that the door was so easily broken into and the look on Jerry's face when she'd done it, he was absolved of this crime, as far as she was concerned. She'd never seriously entertained the notion, but it was good that she could now say without hesitation that he had nothing to do with it.

Just as she had her hand on Double Groove's door, she heard the blatting of the food truck behind her on Robin Circle, and she turned to watch as it pulled into the lot. She took her phone out and pulled up the picture of Keith Bonham she'd taken yesterday. Just in case.

She met the truck as it parked at the end of the building opposite Not Just Vacs. The driver waved at her through the open window. "How ya doin'?" he asked.

"Good, you?"

"Good. We're not open yet, though."

"I know. I work here. I just wanted to ask you a question or two about yesterday."

"The cops already done that. I told 'em I saw a couple of dudes walk around back yestiddy."

Christine showed him the picture. "Was this guy one of them?"

The driver got out of his seat and leaned toward the phone. "Yep," he said without hesitation. "Wished I'da had that pitcher yestiddy, I woulda give it to 'em."

"Could you tell what happened to him after he walked around back?"

"Nope. I seen him walk along that wall, and turn right to go behind the buildin'. Never seen him no more after that."

"Did you happen to notice what time that was?"

"Hmm … musta been around five, maybe quarter after. Just before the big rush started."

"Thanks," Christine said.

Keith Bonham was now her Number One Suspect.

She checked her phone for the time. Just past two o'clock. She had time to dive further into the Bonham rabbit hole before Ronnie arrived.

She called Stella Rineer.

"Hey," Christine said, "You said you were Facebook friends with Keith Bonham's wife?"

"Emily," Stella said. "Yeah, why?"

"I'd like to talk to either her or Keith. I was wondering if you could message her and give her my number."

"Hold on, I'll check her profile. She might even have her number listed on there."

Christine waited.

"Yep," Stella said. She read out the phone number as Christine keyed it into her phone.

"Thanks," Christine said.

"What's up, anyway?"

"Just trying to help the cops do their job. I don't believe their theory that Megan did it."

"Me neither," Stella said. "Good luck."

Christine would have loved to jump right into that call, but she'd just seen two separate handfuls of patrons enter Double Groove as she talked to Stella, and she knew Steven was manning the bar alone right now, with Kyle busy in the back.

She re-entered the taproom and got behind the bar to take beer orders on the B-Side while Steven handled the A-Side. Alice Cooper's *Billion Dollar Babies* was spinning on the turntable.

When Steven and Christine met at the taps the first time, Steven said under his breath, "You think Megan really did it?"

"No. Do you?"

"*Hell* no. You know, they considered me for a hot minute, because of that busted up magic trick. But I was behind the bar the whole time, and there were enough witnesses to prove it."

"What about Brian? Did you see where he was when Scott disappeared?"

"He was outside, sitting at a table on the deck. I saw him there the whole time. But it wouldn't surprise me if it was him all the same, or my aunt, for that matter."

They separated as they served their beers on opposite sides of the taproom, then met again at the taps.

"*What?*" Christine said. "You just said Brian was on the deck. And there's no way your aunt could've done it."

Steven laughed. "That's what she would want you to believe. Ever hear of murder for hire?"

"I ... I actually hadn't thought of that." Now she'd have

to un-eliminate Janis from her list. "But for what reason?"

Back to their respective bars, then Christine went back to the taps one more time, while Steven did some work at the dishwasher. When he was finished, he backed up to be near Christine again. "Listen, I've never really liked Aunt Janis, or either of her husbands, although Brian was a considerable improvement over Scott. There's just so much jealousy and drama over there. Scott fooled around on her while they were married, and they were, like, blood enemies for a few years. Then she married Brian, and things got better, and Brian and Scott even got along with each other for a while. But it never lasts. It's always one of those three stirring up trouble with the other two, like some kind of damn three ring circus. It's so exhausting. I tuned it out a long time ago."

"Why don't you like your aunt?"

"Because she's a user, a manipulator. She plays those two men against each other like you wouldn't believe. Her and my mom never really got along even when they were kids. Mom says Aunt Janis practically invented passive aggressiveness, and believe me, I've seen it in action myself. In fact, I wouldn't put it past her to stage this whole thing just to make herself the victim … which would get publicity … which would drum up sales."

Christine's eyebrows shot up. "Kill somebody for book sales? You're kidding me."

Steven smiled. "I'm not. I'm totally not."

New patrons came in, and Steven took orders while Christine manned the taps. As she stood there watching a pint glass fill with Atomic Blonde, she was reminded of Janis last night, talking about how she'd researched how to get away with murder, and it occurred to Christine that Janis might just be one of the world's leading experts on that particular subject. That stopped her cold.

Could it be?

"And one other thing I bet you didn't know," Steven said, sneaking up on her from behind. "Did you know Scott and Michael knew each other?"

Christine turned around to face him. "Our Michael? Michael Reisinger?"

Steven nodded, still smiling. He was having way too much fun with her.

She passed two beers to their new owners and turned back to Steven. "In what capacity?"

"Not a good one. Scott hit on Michael's wife in a bar one time. In a very hands-on way, the way I heard. To the point where Michael had to step in to defend her. Scott ended up with a broken nose and a concussion, and Michael spent the night in jail."

"Holy crap."

"That's not all. Scott took Michael to civil court after that, and he got some money out of it."

"How much?"

Steven shrugged. "Michael wouldn't say. But he's still pissed about it."

"Wow. Lucky for Michael he was off last night."

Steven smiled again. "Is it?" He turned away and busied himself putting clean glasses back on the shelf.

Christine stopped. Blinked. Shook her head. "No," she said. "Not Michael."

Steven shrugged. "I'm just sayin'."

"Does anybody else know about that?"

He shrugged again. "I haven't told anybody. Except you. But I don't know who else Mike might have told. Or Scott."

Christine sighed. "If it comes out, it comes out," she said, "but for now, let's keep it between us. I'll look into it myself."

CHAPTER TWELVE

WELL, THERE WAS the shadowy Suspect Number Eight she'd been waiting for: Michael, Double Groove's only bartender to have been off duty yesterday.

She couldn't believe it. Michael was a big guy with big hands that she imagined could punish a man's face, but he was about the chillest guy Christine knew. He was a Deadhead, for God's sake. Deadheads never fought, they just spread kindness and bragged about "shows" they'd seen. To an annoying extent, sometimes. Scott's "hands-on" flirting must have bordered on abuse to get Michael to throw a punch.

Still, she knew of two ways to potentially rule him out, and to scratch this itch, she only needed one of them to pan out. She would find out about the first one as soon as Ronnie Gaines came in.

The Alice Cooper album ended, and Steven replaced it with Bob Marley's *Legend*. "One Love" played as Christine served a couple of new customers, and then "I Shot the Sheriff" started.

And as if on cue, in walked Ronnie Gaines.

"Hey, Ronnie."

"Chris." Ronnie nodded and took his customary seat on the B-Side bar.

"What can I getcha?"

"Bang Your Hops, please." Unsmiling, he handed her his card.

Uh-oh, Christine thought. *Is he still mad?* She ran his card, poured him a pint of the hazy, juicy IPA, and brought it to him. "Your new favorite?" she said.

"I like the grapefruitiness of it."

Christine nodded. "It's the citra hops. Good for summer." She watched as Ronnie scanned the room. Several other patrons were scattered around the taproom tables, but all were involved in conversations of their own. One geeky-looking guy, a regular who usually sat alone and had exactly one beer before leaving, was bending Steven's ear on the A-Side. She and Ronnie had the B-Side to themselves, for now.

"So ..." Christine said.

"So, about the investigation," Ronnie said in a low voice. "It's pretty open and shut. Megan was super nervous, but it was easy to tell she really hated the guy. And she kept changing her story. First she said she went for a walk, then she said she was in her car screaming, if you can believe that."

"I do. I told her to do that."

Ronnie looked confused. "What do you mean, you told her to do that?"

"I mean she was upset, and I suggested she go out to her car and scream, you know, to blow off tension. She was a little dubious at first, but in the end, she went for it."

"Why did she lie about it first then?"

"I think she was just embarrassed. It's kind of weird, you know."

Ronnie shrugged. "Anyway. The physical evidence alone

is against her big time. First of all, the autopsy confirmed he was killed by a blow to the base of his skull. Snapped his neck right at that point, and the pipe we found was the weapon that did it. The hair and blood on it were Cornell's, and Megan's prints were on it."

"Along with …"

Ronnie nodded. "Along with yours, and Mark's, and Kyle's."

"Not Michael's?"

"No. Not his."

Christine breathed a silent sigh of relief. Michael, at least, was in the clear. "Could they tell whose prints were the most recent?"

"No. But some of the prints were smeared, as if somebody wearing gloves handled it after they were laid."

Uh-oh. If the killer had been wearing gloves, that brought Michael back into the mix. But still, she remembered that Michael and his wife, Cole, were supposed to have gone to a Billy Strings concert at Pier Six last night. He'd been talking it up for months. In Christine's mind, there was no way he'd have missed it, but she made a note to herself to ask him about the concert the next time she saw him.

Meanwhile, back to the pipe. "Whose prints were smeared?" she asked.

"Everybody but Megan's. But that was because the smears and Megan's prints were at opposite ends of the pipe, so there's no way to tell which was first."

Thinking back, Christine recalled that Megan had held the pipe with her fists at the bent end, with the short arm of the L resting against the bottom of her left fist. A murderer, on the other hand, may have held it at the other end, swinging the bent end, with its flanged lip, in hopes that it would do more damage to a human skull.

Nothing that could get Megan off on the face of it, but it

was definitely something to file away for later. The fact that someone wore gloves meant nothing. They kept boxes of gloves in the production area all the time, for handling corrosive or toxic chemicals. Any one of them could have been the gloved handler. Or it could have been the murderer. Again, nothing conclusive. Just data.

"Anyway," Ronnie continued. "Megan's pretty screwed. It looks like she did it."

"You don't really believe that, do you?"

Ronnie shrugged. "I don't want to, but I have to follow the evidence."

"The evidence tells me that it was either Megan or the gloved person that did it."

"Megan was the only one who had prints on the weapon and a key to the back door of Not Just Vacs, so..."

"That door is pathetically easy to break into. I just did it myself in fifteen seconds. Plus, I'm telling you that I personally spoke to Megan right after the murder, and she was still in her car, and she had no idea a murder had occurred until I told her. Isn't that evidence?"

Ronnie took a sip of his beer and set the glass down. "Christine, we've been through this. You told Kingery about this call, right?"

"Of course."

"And it wasn't enough. It didn't outweigh the physical evidence."

Christine sighed, flailing. "What about Scott's phone? Did they find it?"

"They got the provider to try to ping its location, but nothing came back."

"What does that mean? Whoever took it destroyed it?"

"Possibly," Ronnie said, "but more likely they just turned it off or took out the SIM card."

"And you think Megan did that? And then what? You

didn't find the phone or the SIM card on her, did you?"

"No, and they also searched all the nearby dumpsters and looked up on this building's roof and the two behind it, and all the likely places she could have hidden it or thrown it. But remember, she was gone a long time. Long enough that she could have walked over to 7-Eleven, dropped the phone in the back of somebody's pickup while they were pumping gas, and walked back."

"Oh, come on," Christine said, rolling her eyes.

"It's just an example, and I'm not saying she did that. Just saying she had time to do any number of things to make sure that phone would never be found. And something as tiny as a SIM card? If she put it in the right car, it could be in Miami by now. And that means the fact that we didn't find the phone on her doesn't get her off the hook all by itself."

Christine snorted. "Can they at least find out from the provider who it was that texted him? And when?"

Ronnie nodded. "Yup. You asked me the same question about Megan's phone yesterday, and my answer is the same. We'll have that info in seven to ten days."

Christine shook her head. She couldn't abide the idea of Megan being in jail for another seven to ten days, so effectively, this was another dead end. "I mean, I just don't understand why they're so laser-focused on Megan without even looking at the other suspects."

"They looked at the other suspects. Some of them had motives, some of them had opportunity, but none of them had prints on the murder weapon or a key to the back door. Only Megan had the trifecta of means, motive, and opportunity."

"Did they look at Keith Bonham? The food truck guy said he saw him go behind the building."

"Keith Bonham? The guy Mark banned yesterday?"

"Yeah."

"Why would he wanna kill Scott Cornell?"

"He didn't. I think he wanted to kill Mark, and Mark and Scott look very similar from behind. In fact, when I first saw the body, *I* thought it was Mark for a hot second."

"A hot second is all it takes."

"Exactly," she said, splaying her hands palms up. "Thank you."

Ronnie lifted his brows and tilted his head back and forth. "Huh. That's an angle I hadn't thought of."

"Think you could relay that idea to the powers that be?"

Ronnie nodded. "It's worth looking into."

"Great. In the meantime, while you guys are resting on your laurels, I'm going to keep turning over rocks. Because there's also Brian, and Scott's wife, and even Janis herself, who could have arranged it. There's a lot of bad mojo in that clan."

"Yeah, we know about all that. And there's some other people in Scott's past as well that they looked into, but really … I mean, the evidence."

"Evidence, evidence, evidence. Evidence can be twisted to fit a preconceived notion. And that's what we have here."

"Christine. I know what you're doing here, and I know what you're thinking about doing. All I can say is, be very careful about interfering in an official investigation."

Christine scoffed. "'Official investigation.' You must be kidding me. This is a railroad job, is what it is. They found somebody they like for it, and they're done."

"You don't know what's going on behind closed doors. Don't act like you do. These guys are pros, and they're gonna be as thorough as possible."

"Whatever you say."

"And *don't* tamper with any evidence. Or, for God's

sake, influence witnesses. That could get you in big trouble, bigger trouble than you want, believe me. Just let the pros handle this, Christine."

"The way they've handled it so far?"

Ronnie sat back, frowning. "That's not the only reason to stay out of it," he said. "It could also be dangerous."

"How so?"

"Let's say you're right, and Megan's innocent. That means there's a killer still out there. What if he, or she, gets the idea you're getting too close? They've killed once. They could do it again."

Christine was, in a weird way, okay with this idea. At least he was allowing the possibility that she might be right. She saw this as a step in the right direction. "I'll be careful," she said.

Ronnie stared at his almost empty beer and shook his head. "I made a mistake," he said, "sharing info with you. It stops now." He drained his glass.

"Another?"

Ronnie pushed the glass toward her with an angry curl on his lip. "No. One and done today. Thanks, and remember what I said."

Ronnie settled his tab and walked out the door.

For the next few minutes, Christine smiled and engaged in small talk with other patrons as she served them beers. But inside, she was fuming. How dare he talk to her like that? He actually threatened her! *The nerve.*

He must have forgotten who he was talking to, she thought. Christine knew she had a streak of hardheadedness in her, especially when she thought she was being mansplained, and she was proud of it. The type of tactics Ronnie had employed had virtually guaranteed that she would continue to stick her nose in places it didn't belong.

During a break in the action, she let Steven know that

she'd like to make a phone call, and he nodded his assent. Christine stepped outside and called Emily Bonham. She'd already come up with her story and was ready.

"Hello?"

"Hi, is this Emily?"

"Yes, it is."

"This is Christine Buckley from Double Groove."

Silence.

"I'm not calling to harass you," Christine said. "It's just that we found a wallet out back behind the building yesterday, and it has money in it but no ID. We were wondering if it was Keith's. Would he have any reason to be behind the building?"

"Yeah, he sure would. He doesn't drive. We live on Saddleback Way, right off 543, so he walks behind the building then across to the bypass. What time did you find the wallet? He was home at five-thirty, so he must've left there around five. Keith!" she yelled, away from the phone. "Can you come in here a minute?"

"We found it later, after closing. Are you sure that's when you left?"

"Not me. I left soon after Mark kicked us out. Keith hung around until later, and—"

Christine heard a door close in the background, then heard Keith say, "What's wrong?"

"Do you have your wallet?" Emily said. "They found one at Double Groove, behind the building."

"Really?" Keith said. "I guess it could be mine. I walked home that way."

"No, wait," Emily said. "We went to Taco Bell right after you got home, and you paid, remember? So it can't be your wallet they have."

"Oh, yeah, right," he said. "Nope. Not mine."

"What time were you at Taco Bell?" Christine asked.

"Must've been around quarter to six, six o'clock," Emily said. "Why?"

"Can you prove it? Did you keep your receipt?"

"Why would we need to prove it? Oh, because of that murder over there last night? We were long gone. The receipt's in the trash, but I guess I could dig it out if I had to."

"I would if I were you. You might be hearing from the cops. They're talking to everybody who was here yesterday." *Also*, she thought with a flicker of self-recrimination, *I just sicced 'em on you myself.*

"Okay, thanks for the heads-up. Anyway, it's not Keith's wallet, but thanks for calling."

"Must be someone else's then. Thanks for taking my call."

Christine hung up, dejected. There went the Keith Bonham theory. The Taco Bell receipt would have a time stamp on it, and that would be the end of it. Just to be sure, she looked up Saddleback Way on her Maps app, and sure enough, their story tracked. It would make sense for Keith, a non-driver, to take the shortest path to walk to his home, and that path went behind Double Groove.

Damn, she thought. *I was so sure.*

The only consolation was that there was no one looking over her shoulder at the moment. It was hard enough for her to admit to *herself* when she was wrong, but to admit it to someone else … unthinkable.

But, yeah. I was wrong.

CHAPTER THIRTEEN

THE AFTERNOON BECAME hectic as the patrons poured in. A local blues rock band, Second Wind, set up in the parking lot and started playing, and that brought even more business in. The mood at Double Groove, which had earlier been quiet and almost somber as people spoke in hushed tones about what had gone down yesterday, edged closer and closer to raucous as the day wore on, the sun grew hotter, and the music grew louder. Black Magic Mexican Lager, Crossroads Cream Ale, and Dirty White IPA flew out of the taps like the next day was Doomsday.

During a rare break in the action, Christine snuck off to the brewhouse to call Shane Ritchie. Kyle had long since moved out to the taproom to help out behind the bar, so Christine had the cavernous room to herself.

"Hello?"

"Shane, this is Christine Buckley. I messaged you yesterday?"

"Yeah, I remember. You work at Double Groove, right?"

"That's right."

"Nice place. I prefer Independent, but I've been to the

Groove from time to time. How can I help?"

"A couple things," she said, ignoring the slight. "First I was wondering if you were at the event yesterday, and if so, would you mind sharing any pictures you might have taken?"

"Nah," Shane said. "I really would've liked to be there, but my sister got married yesterday. I was in the wedding party, so I was kind of stuck, but considering how it worked out, I guess I should be glad."

"Oh, well, congratulations to your sister."

"Thanks."

"Nice wedding?"

"Perfect, yeah. Some words, a kiss, pictures, eating, drinking, dancing, the whole kit 'n' kaboodle. Anything else I can do for you?"

"Well, this is a little awkward, but to be frank, I was looking for dirt."

"Dirt?"

"I figured you, as the more-or-less president of Ms. O'Riordan's fan club, might know some behind-the-scenes stories about her circle of associates. Like, does she have any online trolls that worry you? As in, you feel like maybe you should report them? Violent fantasies, and the like?"

"Not that I can think of, off the top of my head. Anyway, nobody tried to kill Janis."

"Yes, but someone may have been trying to hurt her by hurting the people closest to her. And while we're on the subject, how much do you know about the victim and his contacts?"

"I can't think of anybody that would want to hurt Janis," he said. "We've gotten to know each other pretty well through this page and she's a wonderful human being. But as far as Scott Cornell … whoever killed him was doing her a favor, believe me. That guy has always been a slimeball."

"In what way?" she said, leaving alone the fact that Shane's description of Janis conflicted with Steven's. One thing at a time.

"You mean *ways*. First of all, you know he used to work at Chesapeake Brewing and he got caught selling recipes?"

"Yeah," Christine said, "I heard about that. Anything else?"

"Listen, I don't want to be accused of spreading tales. I have a reputation here to keep up. If people start to get the idea I'm dealing in gossip, a lot of my sources will dry up and this fanpage will be orphaned. All I'll say is that you should look into his past. With women … girls, I should say. With businesses. Talk to his widow. I guarantee you, she's not exactly wallowing in grief. And you didn't hear it from me."

Christine sensed that she'd gotten about all she was going to get from him. "Okay," she said, "that's a good start. Thanks for your help."

She hung up and stared into the depths of the brewhouse, lost in thought for a moment or two. While Shane hadn't really said anything definitive, the hints he'd dropped sent a ripple of alarm through her. It was a lot to unpack, but she'd have to do it later. She banished her thoughts and went back to the taproom. The day wasn't over.

***

It being Sunday, Double Groove closed at six o'clock, so Christine got home at a decent hour.

"Mom," Evan said after she'd eaten, "can we go to String Theory tomorrow? I want to get a capo and some new sheet music."

The question set off a daisy chain of free associations in

Christine's mind, and just like that, she figured out the reason Brian Harrison had looked so familiar to her yesterday. It was because Brian Harrison worked at String Theory Cafe, the local music store and coffee bar. She had seen him there several times in the year since Evan first decided to pick up a guitar, and had even been checked out by him a couple of times. Seeing him out of context yesterday, she hadn't been able to make the connection.

This was perfect. She was off the next day, leaving her free to take Evan shopping, and possibly giving her a chance to speak to Brian Harrison in private.

"Yeah," she said, "we can do that."

"Sweet! Thanks, Mom."

That settled, she started loading the dishwasher, and with her mind disengaged, her thoughts drifted back to Scott Cornell.

What Shane had said had been disturbing, to say the least. But with Shane obviously clamming up for understandable reasons, she'd have to find other avenues to dig deeper. She hoped the first step might be Brian Harrison.

"Hey, Chris," her husband called from the living room. "C'm'ere a minute. I think I found somethin'."

Christine started the dishwasher and joined Bobby in the living room, where he sat on the sofa with a laptop. "What's up?"

"I might've found your truck," he said. "Check this out." He turned the laptop toward her as she took the sofa cushion next to him. "It's in Gettysburg, which would mean a day trip, but it might be worth it. Heck, a day trip might be nice, take your mind off all this Double Groove drama for a while. How 'bout tomorrow?"

Christine took the laptop from him and her eyes flicked to the picture of the truck. It gleamed like polished obsidian, with what looked like authentic vintage Cragar mags on it. The front bumper had been removed. Ordinarily she leaned toward historical accuracy, but this particular modification she didn't mind, because it drew attention to the iconic grill design. At least the truck hadn't been lowered.

Christine clicked on the picture to get the truck's specifications. As she scanned down the list, she liked everything she saw, with the exception of the modern five-liter engine with an automatic transmission, but she could work with that.

"Yeah," she said. "This one checks all the boxes, that's for sure. But what was the first thing you noticed about it, Bobby? Besides the picture?"

"Whaddya mean?" He took the laptop back from her, and she pointed to the price tag. It was $20,000 over their pre-established budget.

"Oh," he said. "Didn't notice that. I guess I got blinded by the picture and the specs. So that's a hard no?"

"Yeah, that's a hard no. I want a truck, but I don't want to starve for it." It was discouraging. If this was the going market for what she wanted, it'd be a tough row to hoe finding one at a price they could afford. The website they were on wasn't the best one for deals, but still … $20,000 over. At this rate, she'd be reduced to looking for word-of-mouth deals. Not an impossible task, but one that could take months or years to come to fruition.

"Okay," Bobby said. "We'll keep looking. Somethin'll turn up somewhere."

CHAPTER FOURTEEN

THE NEXT MORNING, Christine fed Mrs. Jingles, and she and the boys departed for String Theory Cafe. For preteen boys, it was bright and early, meaning just past ten o'clock. Christine had already been awake for three hours, and Bobby had long ago left for work.

After a short drive into Bel Air, Christine found a metered parallel parking spot and backed into it like a pro. She and the boys clambered out, and Christine, eschewing the app, went old school and fed the meter with quarters. As they took the sidewalk down Bel Air's quaint historic Main Street, Christine luxuriated in the morning air, admired the hanging petunias, and crossed her fingers in hopes that she would find Brian Harrison at work. They came to String Theory's front door, recessed between angled display windows in a style common to many Main Streets, and as Christine pushed through the door into cool air redolent with the nutty aroma of good coffee, her wish came true.

Brian stood near the back of the store, talking to another customer.

Evan made a beeline for the sheet music and began

browsing, which gave Brian enough time to take his current customer to the register and check him out.

Evan picked out a Beatles songbook and a book of a hundred picking patterns for classic rock, which pleased Christine to no end. She and Bobby had never urged him to focus on any one genre, figuring he'd find his own direction, but somewhere along the way, they must have done something right. Chalk one up for the parents.

Brian came over as they moved toward the capos, and Christine looked up at him and feigned surprise. "Hey!" she said.

"How are ya?" Brian said. "Christine, right?"

"Right. You know, when I saw you Saturday, I couldn't figure out where I knew you from."

Brian laughed. "I get that all the time. Must have one of those faces. You guys need any help over here?"

"I think he found what he wants here," Christine said, "but he needs a capo, too."

"Really?" he said to Evan. "You're too young to learn how to cheat."

"It's not cheating," Evan said, offended.

"I'm just messin' with you. Come over here, I have just the one you need."

As they made their way across the room, Christine said, "Sorry for your loss, by the way."

"Not your fault," Brian said. "We brought our dysfunctionality with us. Something was bound to happen sooner or later."

Christine had been wondering how she was going to steer the conversation into this arena, and now Brian had done it for her. She wasn't ready to go there yet, though. There were formalities to be taken care of first.

"Are you guys holding up okay?"

Brian shrugged. "*I* am, as well as can be expected. Scott

and I haven't been particularly close the past few years, and in fact, he kind of got on my nerves. So I'm fine. Janis is another story."

"She's not doing well?"

He gazed at her for a moment as if gauging how much to divulge. "To be honest," he said, "Janis wasn't doing well to begin with, and this murder is pushing her close to the edge. Don't get me wrong: Scott embarrassed her, so there's probably a part of her that's relieved. But the bigger part of her was still close to him. I mean, he was the father of her child, so …"

"*What?* I had no idea she had children."

"There was only one, her son Lawrence, and he died three years ago. Drug overdose."

Christine hung her head and closed her eyes. "Oh, my God. That's horrible."

"Yes, it was. And Janis hasn't been the same since."

"I understand," she said, gazing at her two boys. "Losing a child is a parent's worst nightmare. I can only imagine what it would do to me."

"If you're anything like Janis, you'd start by self-medicating right away. Cigarettes, booze."

"Cigarettes, never. Booze, probably," she said as they arrived at a display case near the register.

"Here's the capos, my man," Brian said to Evan. "And this is the one I'd recommend for you. Wanna try it out?"

"Sure," Evan said. "I didn't bring my guitar, though."

"We've got a few here," Brian said as he plucked an acoustic guitar off its stand. "Try this one."

Evan took the guitar and the capo and sat on a nearby stool. As he strummed a few chords and then clipped the capo on, Brian continued.

"Janis kicked smoking twenty years ago, but it still made a natural soft place for her to land. The thing that really ate her up was …" He stopped and stared at her as if he'd just realized he was thinking out loud. "I don't know why I'm telling you all this," he said.

"You don't have to. I didn't mean to pry."

"You didn't pry. I volunteered. You have kind eyes, and I don't know why, but I feel like I can trust you not to make this the town gossip. Am I right?"

"Absolutely," Christine said.

"Move the capo closer to the fret," Brian said to Evan. "Right where your finger would be if you were playing a bar chord. You know bar chords?"

"Yes," Evan said as he moved the capo.

"Yes, right there. Good. Janis' big problem," Brian said, turning back to Christine, "was that she blamed herself for Lawrence's death. She knew he had an addiction and, believe me, she did everything she could to help him, but she still felt responsible."

"I would imagine that's not uncommon."

"That's what her therapist says."

"It's good she's seeing someone," Christine said.

"Yes, it is. I'm starting to feel like I should be seeing someone myself," he concluded with a wry smile.

Christine blinked.

"I'm sorry," he said. "I hope you didn't take that as some sort of come-on. It wasn't meant to be. It's just that, over the last few months, things have really gotten super weird in my house, and I'm not dealing with her as easily as I used to be able to."

"Super weird?"

"Yes." He paused, took a breath, and continued. "Out of the blue, she starts worrying about *money*, if you can believe that. We're not filthy rich by any stretch, but we've never had trouble paying the bills, and now, for the last month or so, she's *obsessed* with moving money around, robbing Peter to pay Paul, and so forth. It's all she thinks about, and it's not healthy. So I try to distract her, but whenever I do, she snaps at me."

Christine was quiet, unsure of how to respond. She was a little embarrassed hearing such detail about Brian and Janis' relationship, but at the same time, she did want Brian to talk. She just didn't want to be his therapist.

"I'm really talking too much," Brian continued, apparently feeling as conflicted as Christine. "I apologize. I think maybe I really will look into getting my own therapist," he ended with a chuckle.

The money thing, as awkward as it was to hear about, was interesting. Christine had no idea how much mid-tier writers like Janis made, but somehow she'd had it in her mind that they would be … at least comfortable. Perhaps she'd been naïve.

Say something, she thought. *But keep it neutral.* "I'm so sorry to hear all this, for both of you."

"Thank you," he said. "Keep us in your prayers, if you would. The one good thing is that she still has her writing. When she writes, the world disappears for her. It's the best therapy she has."

"That's good," Christine said. "For her, and for me, too. I've always been a big fan of her work, so I'd hate to see her stop."

Brian smiled. "You and a lot of other people."

"Oh my god," Christine said, finding the tack she wanted to take, "I hope the cops didn't lean on her too hard, given her condition."

Brian's face darkened, his brow pinched in anger. "They actually did, and it's set her back big-time. Can you believe they treated her like a suspect? Janis wouldn't kill a fly if it landed on her sandwich and gave her the finger, and I *told* them that. Still, they grilled her like an Oscar Meyer

Wiener. I mean, did they not notice she was behind the lectern when he died?"

Christine nodded. "I have my own problems with the way they've been handling things."

"Oh?"

Her seed was planted. Time to water it. "The person they arrested? That was my friend Megan, and I know for a fact she didn't do it. But they think they've got their killer, and I think they've stopped investigating."

Brian's eyes grew wide. "That means the real killer ..."

"Is still out there," she finished for him.

"My god," he said. "He could kill again." His eyes darted around the room.

Harvest time. "We need to figure out who it was, before that happens. You knew Scott. Can you think of anybody else who might have had it in for him?"

Evan sat behind them, happily strumming. Kyle, on the other hand, was starting to get antsy. "Mommmmmm ..." he said in a whiny voice.

"Just a minute," she said to her older son.

"I'll tell you what I told the police," Brian said. "You should talk to his wife. Janis and I both think he'd been having an affair, and if she found out about it ..."

Christine nodded. "Trouble." This was exactly the kind of thing she'd been hoping to unearth.

"Yes. But what if it's got nothing to do with that? What if it's somebody that really wants to harm my wife? Could someone be trying to hurt her by hurting those closest to her?"

"I mean ..."

"They might come for her next. Or me. Dear God, this is just too much."

"Brian," she said. "Settle down. I know it's scary, but if we work together, we can figure this out. Would you know of anybody like the person you just described?"

Brian, still rattled, blew out a breath. "Not personally, but in every fanbase there are some sickos, know what I mean? The guy to ask about that would be Shane Ritchie."

"I already talked to him, and he wasn't very helpful on that front. I'll circle back to him if you think I should, but to be honest, I'm more interested in looking into Scott's past, and I think the best person to ask about that is your wife. Do you think she'd be willing to talk to me?"

Brian stared at her, the moment of silence stretching through several heartbeats. "It wasn't entirely a coincidence," he finally said, "that you dropped in here today, was it?"

Christine smiled. "Not entirely. Evan did beg me to come in for a capo, that's the truth. I guess maybe I was hoping for a little ... serendipity? And I got it."

"And your real interest in all this is saving your friend Megan?"

"Yes. As I said, I don't think she's guilty, and I feel like the cops are kind of focusing on her because it's the easy way out."

"How do I know you're not looking to scapegoat somebody to get Megan off the hook?"

"I would never do that. I want to find the real killer, and your wife has been through enough. I wouldn't do anything to upset her further. It's just that I think she can help."

Brian nodded. "Okay. I guess I believe you."

"So ..."

"I really don't know if she'll talk to you, though. She's a bit on the reclusive side to begin with, and after the other night ... you have no idea. But I'll tell you what. I'll mention it to her, and I'll get back to you if you leave me your number. I don't promise anything, but I'll do my best to convince her it's important."

"Because it is. We want to get this guy off the streets."

He nodded. "I get that. Although I'm going to try to convince her without bringing that part up, if I can."

"I appreciate it. It's all I can ask."

"Also, I will say it would be best if you don't bring up the fact that you're a big fan. That'll get her hackles up right away."

"Not a problem," she said, and she mimed zippering up her mouth.

Brian exhaled again. "Sorry I sort of lost the thread back there."

"Don't be sorry. It was understandable. Truth be told, you seem to be holding up pretty well yourself."

"Outside of being scared out of my wits? And overly talkative?"

Christine laughed. "I'm serious. All things considered, I don't know how you're handling this with such poise. With all this going on, and to have you and your wife labelled suspects at the same time."

"Oh, I'm not a suspect anymore."

"Really? I'm sorry, I just assumed. You know, those closest …"

"Listen, I'm a musician, don't forget. I tune guitars for a living. I love a live show more than anything, so I left the book reading early to get a good seat for the Willig Boys. I was out there the entire time, and there were plenty of witnesses."

Christine nodded. One of those witnesses would be Jeff Willig, who was also on the deck the entire time. Brian's story gibed with what Steven had told her, but Steven had been in and out and couldn't attest to Brian's *continuous* presence out there. Jeff could, and Christine would ask him at the earliest opportunity. "That's good to hear," she said. "You also mentioned I should talk to Tina. Would you be willing to give me contact info for her as well?"

Brian nodded. "Of course. Be careful with her, though."

"I'll be as respectful as I can be."

"You misunderstand. You don't have to worry about Tina, she's about as endearing as a porcupine. I meant be careful for yourself. If you want, I can give her a heads-up, kind of grease the skids for you."

Christine thought about it a moment. "Thanks, but I don't think so. If it's all the same to you, I'd rather catch her off guard."

Brian shrugged. "It's your ball game."

∗ ∗ ∗

A few minutes later, as they exited String Theory Café, Christine told Kyle, "Now we can go to Target and get you that R/C monster truck."

"Yay!" Kyle said. "But can we go look at comics first?"

"Yeah," Evan said. "I wanna go to the record store, too."

Since the record store was right next door, they made a brief stop in there, and Evan got a used vinyl LP of *Led Zeppelin III*. Then they crossed the street, and each of the boys picked out a few new comic books.

Both boys' noses were in their comics as Christine pulled out of the parking spot.

Brian had been a fantastic witness, not too hard to crack open and full of information, once she'd supplied the proper motivation. She was starting to think she might be good at this.

She'd learned a lot from Brian, and gotten some leads to explore further. On the way to Target, Christine wondered for the first time if she should expand her list of suspects, not only into those trying to hurt Janis O'Riordan indirectly

… but also into unknown entities hoping to indirectly do harm to Double Groove itself, through association with a high-profile murder.

And again, what had Scott been doing in the brewhouse in the first place? She'd been assuming that the police were right when they said he'd received a text luring him back there, especially with the missing cell phone lending credence to that theory. But what if he'd been up to something? Could he have been looking to cash in on some of Mark's recipes?

On the way home from Target, Christine got a text from Megan.

> **Megan:** Just wanted to lyk im home and im ok. I dont wanna talk yet but i heard what ur doing and ily for it {Heart emoji}

> **Christine:** Hang in there gurl we got you {Heart emoji}

CHAPTER FIFTEEN

AFTER A QUICK lunch at home, as Evan sat in his room practicing guitar and Kyle jumped his new monster truck over hastily-built cardboard ramps in the back yard, Christine relaxed in the living room to gather her thoughts.

First, she went over her constantly shifting rogues' gallery of suspects. She'd already ruled out Megan, Lisa, Steven, Keith Bonham, Jerry McKernan, and Brian Harrison. That left five.

One: Mark. She didn't want to think it, but she couldn't in good conscience rule him out until she could establish his whereabouts during the critical time. His motive: unknown, but probably having to do with Scott's history as a recipe thief and/or his kicking of the dog.

Two: Tina Cornell. She too had disappeared at the wrong time, and she may have had multiple reasons to kill her husband, but her physical dimensions and manner of dress that night argued in her favor. Christine had plans to either pin her or rule her out later today.

Three: Janis O'Riordan. Despite Brian's insistence that she hadn't the stomach for murder, she still could have been involved through a proxy. Her apparent state of near emotional collapse did nothing to help her case, and the revelation of her recent money worries was disturbing to Christine. She would have to dig deeper into that at some point.

Four: Michael. Another one she didn't really want to consider, but until she had a chance to engage him about the concert he'd supposedly attended Saturday night, he remained on the list.

Five-A: The mysterious unknown suspect. Scott, by all accounts, had been a singularly unlikable fellow, and for all she knew may have had enemies lined up to knock him off, for any number of reasons. She would shed more light on that later today or tomorrow, she hoped.

Five-B: Alternatively, the mysterious unknown suspect may also have been trying to hurt Janis, hurt Double Groove, or kill Mark.

Christine shook her head. Despite the fact that she had clearly narrowed things down, it still felt wide open to her. There was still a lot of work to do.

It was time to place a phone call.

* * *

Two hours later, Christine was on the move again. She had let the boys know that she'd be out for an hour or so, and they had both waved at her without so much as turning to face in her direction.

Christine stopped at the local edible fruit shop and picked up her order, a sympathy arrangement that she'd requested earlier by phone. Then she put Tina's address into the Highlander's GPS. She'd considered calling ahead to make sure Tina was at home, but didn't want to give her a chance to leave, or simply refuse to answer the door. Christine figured her chances of finding Tina at home were pretty good, and went with it.

A twelve-minute drive found her in a housing development that had probably been in vogue a generation or two earlier but was now showing some signs of shabbiness, in both the conditions of the homes and the overgrowth of trees and shrubs. She parked in the cracked concrete driveway of a modest split-foyer, exited her car, and knocked on the door.

Seconds later, she heard the thumping of feet on stairs from within, and the door opened to reveal Tina, standing on the landing between the home's two floors.

"Oh. Hi," Tina said, blinking.

"Hi Tina. I'm Christine, from Double Groove."

"I remember."

"I just wanted to let you know that we at Double Groove are thinking about you, and to drop off this arrangement."

"Oh, it's so pretty!" Tina said. "Almost too pretty to eat. Would you like to come in for a minute?"

"I don't want to take up too much of your time. I know you must be busy."

"Psssh. Busy ain't the word. I could use a break, to be honest. Please, come on in." She held the storm door open for Christine, who noticed that Tina had taken time this morning to do her makeup. Her lips had that comically plumped-up sex doll look that was considered attractive by some, but to Christine, she just looked like she'd been punched in the mouth.

"Well, okay. Thank you." Christine stepped through the door and handed Tina the fruit arrangement, which was built to resemble a bouquet of flowers. "I'm so sorry for your loss, Tina."

"Thank you. I can't tell you what a pain in the ass it's been. I've been on the phone all morning. Funeral home, lawyers, relatives .... Total buzzkill. Would you like a drink? I'm having gin and tonic."

What the ...? Christine thought. She knew people processed grief in different ways, but this woman acted like no bereaved widow she'd ever heard of. "Do you have any bottled water?" she said.

"Sure," Tina said as she preceded Christine up the half-flight to the living/dining/kitchen area. Christine couldn't help but notice that Tina had a butt she would kill for. Tina was either two to three decades younger than Scott, or extremely well preserved, and she had on short shorts and a tank top, the better to show off her tight tanned skin.

Christine, painfully aware of her forty-one years, tamped down her inner cattiness and tried not to be too judgmental. It wasn't a crime to be young and beautiful.

"Have a seat," Tina said when they reached the top of the stairs. As Christine lowered herself onto the sofa, Tina placed the fruit arrangement on the breakfast bar between the dining room and kitchen and went to the refrigerator.

She came back to the living room with her own glass in one hand and a bottle of water in the other, and handed the bottle to Christine.

"Thanks."

"Not a problem," Tina said. She tossed a lustrous wave of straightened blonde hair over her shoulder as she took a seat in an armchair facing Christine. She settled herself, crossed her legs, looked at Christine, and said, "I went home with Mikey Karavas that night. We left just after five o'clock, and we were together all night. I didn't even find out Scott was dead until the morning."

Christine blinked. "Um. Okay. Did anybody from the Sheriff's Office contact you yet?"

"Yes, and I told them the same thing."

"Okay. Well, that's good to know. Thanks." The first

question she'd had in mind, of course, was whether Tina herself had an alibi, but Tina had blurted it out unsolicited, and Christine appreciated having been relieved of the responsibility of asking.

"I figured you weren't here just to deliver edible flowers," Tina said. She ended almost every sentence with a Valley-Girl vocal fry.

"You're right," Christine said. "I'm here because I don't think Megan killed your husband, and I want to find out who did. I wanted to ask you if you knew of anyone else who might've wanted to do that."

"Psssh. Are you serious? There's a whole list of women that would qualify. But if I were you, I'd talk to Charlie Hawkins."

"Hold up. What whole list of women?"

"We had, I guess, what you'd call an open marriage. He had his flings, I had mine. We didn't interfere with each other's urges. It's healthy."

There went the motive, Christine thought. It was looking like she could scratch Tina off her list of suspects. But she sensed a data trove here, and she wanted to mine it.

"But a few of his flings," Tina continued, "got a little … let's say possessive. Did you know Mikey moonlights as an adult film star?"

The non sequitur had come out of Tina's mouth like she'd earned some sort of medal. Christine restrained herself from rolling her eyes. "No, he doesn't," she said. "He and Mark made up that story to impress one of his girlfriends, and it just went viral. It was Mark that named him Stumpgrinder. I was there that day."

"Oh." She pouted. She *actually pouted*.

"Can we get back to Scott's flings that were jealous?"

"Possessive," Tina said. "Not jealous."

"Fine. Possessive then. Were any of them 'possessive'

enough to want to kill him for straying?"

"As if," she said with a giggle. "Kill *me*, maybe."

"How about *your* flings? Were any of *them* 'possessive' enough to want to kill your husband?"

"Nah. I'm always up front with them that I'm married and there can't be any attachment. It's just sex."

"Impressive. You have a code of ethics."

"Right? Honesty is the best policy."

Christine immediately regretted her kneejerk sarcastic comment. Fortunately, it had gone over Tina's head. She had no wish to antagonize her witness, but to Christine, who had married her high school sweetheart and remained faithful to him for two decades, Tina was like a creature from another planet.

Although Tina's values didn't align with Christine's, one line of questioning had just evaporated because of them. Christine knew women like Tina existed, and she knew some men were attracted to them, but those men had to be as shallow as she was ... and therefore unlikely to be willing to kill for her. They'd simply move on to the next hook-up.

"What about this other guy you mentioned? Charlie something?"

"Hawkins. Charlie Hawkins. He was Scott's business partner until about five years ago."

"What kind of business?"

"They flipped houses," Tina said. "But there was some kind of falling out. I don't know the details, but there was *serious* bad blood between them afterward. I mean screaming, threats, lawyers, the whole nineteen yards."

"Nine."

"Huh?"

"The whole nine yards," Christine said.

"That's what I said."

"Who was doing the threatening?" Christine said.

"Both of them."

Now *this* sounded interesting.

"Do you, by any chance," Christine said, "have Mr. Hawkins' number?"

"I don't know," she said, taking her phone from her hip pocket with considerable effort. "If I still had Scott's phone, I could tell you for sure, but it's gone, and the stupid cops took his laptop—wait. Here it is. I'll text it to you."

Christine gave Tina her number, then waited until she felt her phone vibrate in her own pocket, then said, "Got it. Thanks."

"Not a problem. I hope you nail the prick."

"Well," Christine said, rising from her seat, "I don't want to take up any more of your time. I know you've got relatives to call and so forth."

"Don't remind me. Thanks for dropping by. I really appreciated the break."

"You're quite welcome. Call me if you need anything."

"Thanks, I will," Tina said. "Hey, you know? You're kinda hot for your age. You're married, right?"

"Yeah, why?"

"You ever think about a threesome?"

CHAPTER SIXTEEN

A SHUDDER OF revulsion rippled down Christine's back as she walked back to her car, leaving Tina Cornell to deal alone with the inconvenience of losing her husband.

She could easily confirm Tina's alibi, and she would, just to be sure. But while Tina was certainly not innocent by any stretch of the imagination, Christine had to admit she was almost certainly innocent of Scott's murder.

Before backing out of Tina's driveway, she shot a quick text to Mark, asking him to forward her Mikey Karavas' contact. She didn't wait for a reply, figuring she'd pick it up at her next stop.

Unlike Tina, whom she considered a long shot and only wanted to definitively rule out by confirming with Mikey, in Charlie Hawkins she sensed a solid lead.

On the road, she called to check up on the boys—they were fine—and wasted no time after that placing a call to Mr. Hawkins.

"Hawkins Enterprises, may I help you?"

"I was hoping to speak to Charlie; is he available?"

"This is Charlie. What can I do for ya?"

"Hi, Charlie, this is Christine Buckley from Double

Groove Brewing."

"Hah! Where Scott Cornell got what he had coming, right?"

"It's where he was murdered, yes. I assume you've already talked to the police?"

"You betcha," he said. "Told 'em everything I knew, man, which wasn't much. Haven't seen the bastard in years, or cared to."

"This might sound strange, but I was wondering if you knew of anybody, besides yourself, who …"

"Might've wanted to whack him?" He laughed. "It wasn't me, if that's what you're getting at. Don't get me wrong, man; I'm glad he's dead. I guess you know what went on between us?"

"Not really," Christine said.

"We had a company together. We bought old dilapidated houses, fixed 'em up, and sold 'em for profit. He was the money guy, I was the contractor. I did the framing, the roofing, the drywall, plumbing, electrical, HVAC, all of it. And I'm good. I don't take any shortcuts, man, I do every house like I was gonna live in it myself. Deal was, he'd buy the place, I'd put in the work, buy all the materials, pay my crew, and when the house was sold, we'd take my expenses off the top, then split the proceeds. But like a dummy, I didn't get it on paper, man. Thought a handshake would take care of it."

"But it didn't."

"For the first three houses, it did. Not on the fourth. Never got a dime from him on that one. His name was on the deed, so he pocketed it all, and I didn't have anything on paper, so I got screwed. I lost everything, man. My credit, my company, my house. Not to mention my wife. I had to move into a shithole apartment in somebody's basement."

"And he laughed all the way to the bank."

Charlie snorted. "Not exactly. He used it to pay off his home equity loan, which he had maxed out on gambling debts."

"Ah. What did he gamble on?"

"Everything, man. Sports, horses, casinos. He'd gamble on the color of Taylor Swift's underwear if he had a way to find out what it was."

"And after he paid off that loan, he could gamble again."

"You got it, sister. It's been six years now, he's prob'ly got it about maxed out again. Meanwhile, I'm just now starting to rebuild my life, got this little home improvement gig going, just me and one helper."

"Whew," Christine said. She should have been shocked, but given what she'd learned about Scott Cornell in the past couple of days ... she wasn't. "I can understand why the cops wanted to talk to you."

"Yeah, me too. But luckily, I was in Ocean City all weekend, man, and I had the receipts. Anyways, I'm glad you called, because the cops asked me the same question you did, and at the time I was totally focused on making sure I didn't get my ass tossed in jail, so I didn't think about this until after they left."

"Think about what?" she said.

"You prob'ly heard he leaves a string of heartbroken women behind him, right?"

"Yeah, kind of." *Women?* Yes, but *heartbroken?* Hard to believe.

"Did anybody mention anything about the one girl that was, let's say, a little on the fresh side?"

Zing. In a flash, Christine recalled an offhand comment made by Shane, the fan club guy. Something about girls as opposed to women. She'd chalked it up as a verbal gaffe at the time and forgotten about it ... until now. "How fresh?"

"Seventeen, I think. Still in high school, for sure. Her dad was awful pissed, man, you shoulda seen him. He busted into our shop one day and started whalin' on Scott, man. I had to step in and break it up before Scott got knocked out, but he still walked away with a black eye and a busted lip."

"Was there a police report or anything?"

"No. The dude just left, and they dropped it. Got it out of their systems, I guess."

So the police wouldn't even know about it, Christine thought. "How long ago was this?"

"I remember I was workin' on that fourth house I told you about, the drywall had just gone up, so I'm gonna say … more than six years, less than seven."

"Do you happen to remember the guy's name?"

"No idea. Never saw him again. But I know the girl's name. Scott was real proud of himself, man, so he bragged about his teenage girlfriend all the time. Her name was Bethany Fry."

"That's very helpful, thanks. I won't take up any more of your time. Thanks for talking to me, Charlie."

"No problem, man. If you need windows, or new flooring, new cabinets, anything like that … gimme a holler."

"I might just."

On her way home, Christine's mind went into overdrive, and it had nothing to do with '41 Ford Trucks.

Fry. Fry. Something about that name tugged a thread in her memory. Who did she know with that last name? Somebody ….

She teased at the thread for a few moments, and an image popped into her head. Tall guy, mid-forties, brown hair, weak chin, full mustache. She could see him.

A shock ran through her.

The thread had led to *Randy Frey. Frey,* not *Fry.* Different spelling, same pronunciation.

Charlie had spoken the name, not spelled it, so Christine's mind had supplied the spelling, and if she was on target with her thinking now, it had supplied the *wrong* spelling.

Randy Frey. Not quite a regular, but certainly a returning customer at Double Groove. She'd run his card herself a few times.

Could it be? He seemed about the right age to have a daughter in her early twenties, and he had the right name.

And he had been present that evening. Christine had seen him in the taproom herself. She hadn't paid attention to him throughout the night, so she didn't know how long he'd been there, but she'd seen him arrive just before the book release party started.

When she arrived at home, she peeked in on the boys, who were right where she'd left them, and checked to see if Mark had answered her query.

He had, providing Mikey Karavas' contact info without any accompanying smart-aleck comments. Would wonders never cease.

She had a couple of things to do now. Call Mikey Karavas, find out if Randy Frey had a daughter named Bethany, and get something happening for dinner. Lucky for her, she could multitask. As she took onions, green peppers, and andouille sausage from the fridge and laid them out on a cutting board, she placed the call to Mikey.

"Yeah," Mikey said, a trace of pride in his voice, "she was with me all night. She bang bang long time, know what I mean?"

"Okay, that was more than I needed to know, but thanks."

"She thinks I'm a porn star," he said with a laugh. "She's

been texting me ever since, too, but I'm ghosting her. She's too hung up on herself."

"Thanks, Mikey. See you at the Groove."

Well, that was that. Christine could stop thinking about Tina.

She sliced the sausage and put it in a pan with some olive oil. As it sautéed, she sliced the peppers and onions and pressed two cloves of garlic.

As for Charlie Hawkins, that was another story. She supposed he could still be considered a suspect, technically, but in her mind, Christine had already filed him away under "To Be Investigated If All Other Leads Crash and Burn," with Janis and Brian. While she was not an expert, she had found his reaction to be authentic. And at the risk of typecasting, she had read him as the guy you wanted installing your new kitchen, but not the kind of guy who was savvy enough to put on a good show like that if he harbored any feelings of guilt.

After the sausage, she sautéed the vegetables, then put the whole mess, along with some chicken broth, cajun seasoning, white rice, a can of roasted red peppers, and a pound of shrimp in the pressure cooker, stirred it, closed it up, and started the timer for four minutes.

On to Randy Frey. She leaned back against the kitchen counter and opened the Facebook app on her phone. She navigated to Double Groove's page, and searched their list of followers for Randy Frey. Found him. Opened his profile. Went to his About info. Checked his Family members.

Douglas Frey, Son. Aaron Frey, Son. Nancy Sturgill, Sister. Colton Sturgill, Nephew.

Bethany Frey. Daughter.

Cue the *Psycho* strings.

The next thing was to establish his timeline. She went

back to the Double Groove page, and searched for pictures of the event. Found Randy, in a single picture from before the party started. She knew it was before the party because Strazz was in the same picture, and she was almost certain Strazz had left once Janis started reading. It didn't mean Randy had also left early, it just meant she didn't have any photographic proof that he'd lingered. Yet.

She hadn't yet heard from Brian Harrison, either, and she wondered if that meant bad news. Had Brian forgotten to bring it up with his wife when he'd come home from work, or had he brought it up as promised, only to be rebuffed?

Christine figured he would have let her know what Janis said either way, so she was leaning toward the first option. Brian had yet to ask his wife about talking to Christine, either because he forgot, or he was waiting for the proper time.

Oh, well. There was no point rushing it. She had to trust Brian to handle this delicate situation the right way, and it would happen when it happened. Or it wouldn't happen, and there wasn't much she could do about it either way.

In fact, did she really need Janis anymore? She was feeling pretty good about the Randy Frey lead. She could almost smell the end of her quest, and until that lead petered out, who cared about what Janis might have to say?

She moved to the living room, sat down with Kyle, and flicked on the TV with a huge sigh. She'd spent most of the day following a chain of suspects that kept getting ruled out, until the Randy Frey thing came up, and she wasn't sure about him either. She'd have to find either corroborative or exculpatory evidence before she could move on to the next link in the chain, if there was one.

But not today. She'd done her best, and was proud of what she'd accomplished, but she was now officially burnt out. The pressure cooker would take care of itself.

Mrs. Jingles hopped onto her lap and curled up into a ball. Christine stroked the cat's fur and closed her eyes...

* * *

Her eyes snapped open when she heard the back door slam. Bobby had arrived home from work.

Christine and Bobby allowed the boys to take their dinner to the living room and eat in front of the TV, granting themselves a modicum of privacy as they recapped their respective days. Bobby's had been busy but prosaic, so he went first. Christine's had been ... unusual ... and took a good bit longer to tell about than Bobby's.

"So do you think this guy Randy really did it?" Bobby asked.

"I hope so," Christine said as she went back to the pressure cooker for a refill. "Otherwise, I'm back to Mark being the culprit ... which means I'm back to the drawing board."

"Or Janis or her husband could have hired somebody, or this guy Hawkins could have snuck in the back door."

"Yeah, those are all back-burner possibilities. I'm hoping to get a chance to talk to Janis soon, and maybe I can get a read on whether she had some kind of long-standing vendetta against him. But right now, this guy Randy Frey needs to be ruled out or ruled in, one or the other. I'm gonna talk to Strazz tomorrow, find out if he knows when Randy left. If I can establish that he was still there at the time of the murder, I guess I'll ... actually, I don't know what the next logical step would be."

"The next logical step," Bobby said, pointing at her with his fork, "would be to let the cops know what you found out, and back off."

"You sound like Ronnie Gaines."

"That's because we're both right. Also," he added with a smirk, "we have similar taste in women."

"Hilarious," Christine said. "The thing is, I don't know if I trust the cops. I told you about this guy Kingery."

"But if you present him with overwhelming evidence … which if the story you told me about Randy checks out, it definitely qualifies … then he won't be able to ignore it. Megan could get off on reasonable doubt, and Kingery would know that."

"Maybe …"

Christine's text message ringtone sounded from her phone. She pulled it out of her pocket. "Speak of the devil," she said.

"What, Randy Frey texted you?"

"No, Strazz did." She grew quiet, then a smile crept across her face as she read.

Strazz: Hey my brother knows Somebody thats selling a 41 ford truck. Is that the year ur looking for?

Christine: Yes. What kind of shape is it in and how much does he want

Strazz: Real good shape I'll send a pic. Idk what he wants for it appar he hasnt listed it anywhere yet I'll shoot you his number if you want

Christine: Plz and thx

The picture came through next, and her heart leapt. The truck was a joy to behold. Paint and chrome gleaming brightly, no signs of cancer that Christine could see. Looked mostly original or a really good deep fake.

The seller's contact info came in the following text.

This could be the one she'd been looking for. Word of mouth sales were generally cheaper than those listed on the big online sites or found at car shows. But before showing the truck to Bobby, she sent another text to Strazz.

Christine: It's a stunner. TY

Strazz: Np

Christine: Off topic Q – Sat night, did you notice if Randy Frey was still there when you left?

Strazz: No he went to Ironbirds game he walked out right before me

Christine: Any chance he was faking

Strazz: Wdym

Christine: Did he really leave, or could he have snuck back later if he did

Strazz: You thinking he mightve killed that guy? {laughing emoji} No way why would he do that

Christine: They have history

Strazz: Wow ok. Id be surprised but who knows. Anyway i saw him get in his car and leave

Christine: I'll check out his alibi

Strazz: Lol ok miss marple

Christine: Lol stfu this is for Megan

Strazz: Understood. Go get em vike. Anything I can do to help, just ask

Christine: Thx, and thx again for the lead on the truck I'll call him

Strazz: {Thumbs up emoji}

Christine sighed. Another dead end, most likely. She would check out that alibi, but for now she had to assume Randy was in the clear. "Randy went to the Ironbirds game that night, according to Strazz," she told her husband.

"Another one bites the dust."

"Looks that way. But get this, Strazz also sent me a picture of this truck." She handed the phone to Bobby. "It belongs to a friend of Strazz's brother, and the guy wants to sell it. What color would you call that, anyway? Burnt orange? Cinnamon?"

"Copper," Bobby said.

"Copper. Yeah, that's it. I'm gonna call him. Wanna go see it tonight, if he's available?"

Bobby frowned. "I don't know, babe. This isn't an original color."

"So?"

"Plus ... if this is the same truck ... is the guy selling it named Julius something?"

"Yeah, how did you know?"

"I looked at this truck a couple weeks ago, and it's not

what it seems. The motor's an old 327, not in good shape. The undercarriage is mostly rusted out. The interior's a mess, and it needs a new drive shaft."

"Where was I when you looked at it?"

"It came up through a guy I work with. We checked it out on company time, and I never told you about it 'cause it didn't pan out."

"Oh." She paused for thought. "I'd still like to see it myself, though. Maybe he'll come down on his price."

Bobby sighed. "How about tomorrow, then? It's not listed, so there's no real rush, and I'm really beat."

Christine fumed. What was wrong with him? "I don't care if it's listed or not, that truck could be gone by tomorrow."

"It won't be," he said. "Trust me."

"Fine," she said. "Tomorrow."

But she wasn't happy.

Another text came in. This time it was from Brian Harrison.

> **Brian:** Janis would like to meet you for coffee tomorrow at String Theory. Can you make it?
>
> **Christine:** What time?
>
> **Brian:** 9:00?
>
> **Christine:** Absolutely. Tell her thanks and I'll see her then.

CHAPTER SEVENTEEN

TUESDAY MORNING. DOUBLE Groove was closed again, so Christine had the day off. When she got up at eight o'clock, Bobby had already left for work. The kids were still asleep. It was seventy-eight degrees and sunny.

On a morning like this, she would ordinarily have made herself a cup of coffee and gone outside to drink it in the shade, while watching the goldfinches and hummingbirds swarm their respective feeders. But she had plans to go to a coffee shop to meet Janis, so she settled for watching the birds *without* coffee. It went a little against the grain, but she managed.

At eight-forty-five, the boys were still asleep, so she left them a note. If they woke up before she returned, they knew where to find the cereal.

Nine o'clock found her walking through the door of String Theory Café once again, not quite twenty-four hours after her last visit. Although the café had been open for a couple of hours, the music store portion had just opened, and Christine passed Brian, turning on lights behind the counter. He saluted her with two fingers as she continued to the back of the store. He crooked his finger at her, and she met him at the counter.

"Please don't mention anything about the money," he said quietly. "If she finds out I told you about that, I'm a dead man."

Christine raised an eyebrow.

"Poor choice of words," Brian said, laughing. "You know what I mean. I'll be in big trouble."

Christine smiled. "I'll keep it to myself." Inside, she was disappointed. It was one of the things she'd wanted to talk to Janis about, but she would honor Brian's wish … unless Janis brought it up.

She smelled the café first. Next, she heard it, as an espresso machine whined, and finally she saw the sectioned-off area as she turned a corner to the right at the rear of the store.

Christine's eyes widened in pleasant surprise. The little room was maybe five hundred square feet, tops. Chocolate-colored walls with raised panel wainscoting and five small café tables, each with either two or four simple bentwood chairs. A short coffee bar with a single barista working behind it. Besides Christine, two customers were currently taking advantage of this impossibly cute café, one of whom was at the counter waiting for his espresso, and the other of whom was Janis O'Riordan, sitting alone at a corner table with a steaming cup, reading her phone screen. She looked up at Christine's entrance, smiled, and waved. "Hi," Christine said, smiling back.

Christine approached the counter and ordered a medium hazelnut coffee. She added cream and sugar to it, then took it to the table to join Janis. She sat down and took a sip. "Oh, that's good."

"Yes," Janis said, "I've never come away from here dissatisfied, unlike that pretentious corporate-owned millennial-magnet over on Baltimore Pike, whose name we shall not mention."

"You mean the one with the green logo?"

"Is it green? I barely noticed." Janis was sensibly dressed in a sundress and rattan sandals, her makeup light and tasteful, her reading glasses perched on the end of her nose, her smile genuine and rather disarming. Christine found herself warming to this version of Janis O'Riordan, despite what she'd previously heard from others, including Janis' nephew, and despite the snap opinion Christine had formed herself on the night of the reading. Perhaps the crowd at Double Groove had made her come off as prissy and standoffish, and this was the real Janis. Christine hoped so. "What are you having?" she asked.

"Vanilla latte. And yours is hazelnut, if my nose doesn't lie to me."

"You guessed it."

"So how can I help you?" Janis said.

"First of all, I want to thank you for seeing me. I know this is a difficult time for you and your family."

Janis waved off her comment. "Brian told me why you're doing this, and we both support you. However I can help."

Christine was fascinated by Janis' eyes. They were so blue that she wondered if they might be artificially enhanced. Time had softened her features, but Janis must have been stunning in her twenties and thirties. "I appreciate it, truly," Christine said. "The thing you can help me with most is understanding more about Scott. If you wouldn't mind sharing about the years you were married to him, and anyone you may have noticed who might have had a grudge …"

Janis sighed deeply as she took off her readers and let them drop onto her chest, where they hung suspended from the tether around her neck. "Scott left a trail of grudges behind him like breadcrumbs," she said. "But we've been divorced for more than twenty years now, so you realize we're going way back."

Christine nodded. "I understand that. Still, I'd like to know. Any little thing could end up being the trigger that breaks something open. I spoke to Shane about it the other day, but he wasn't able to help me much."

"Who?"

"Shane Ritchie?" Christine said. "The guy that runs your fan page on Facebook?"

"Oh, *him*. The little basement-dweller."

Christine was taken aback. "I was under the impression that the two of you had grown quite close. Was I wrong about that?"

Janis burst out laughing. "I bet I know who gave you that impression."

"Um … yeah, I guess it was Shane. So it's a one-way street, I take it?"

"That's one way of putting it. He's a fame chaser. Not that I'm famous, or anything, but for some reason, he gets his own sense of self-esteem from pretending to be my friend."

"Hm," Christine said. "A little creepy."

"Maybe, I suppose, but he's harmless, and he does his job. He drives traffic to my books, and solicits reviews, and so forth, so I look at our relationship as symbiotic."

Christine smiled. "I understand," she said. Although she'd spent the ride from her house coaching herself not to get overwhelmed by the fact that she'd be having coffee with one of her favorite authors, she now found that it had been unnecessary. Janis was just a person, and Christine found it easy to interact with her as simply a person. "But the bottom line is," she continued, "I didn't get much information from him about Scott's past, which I suppose should be no surprise, and that's why I came to you."

"I'm afraid you won't get much from me either," Janis said. She took a sip of her latte before continuing. "Listen, I blame myself. I married him. I didn't recognize the fact that he was playing a part until he stopped playing it, and by then it was too late. The upshot of it all is, I really don't know much about him. We were married for almost nine years, and in that time, I don't think I ever figured out who Scott really was, other than a narcissist. Soon after our son was born, I did begin to realize that he wasn't who I'd *thought* he was, and by the time Lawrence was walking on his own, I'd ceased to care whether Scott lived or died. I had my son, and I had my writing, and Scott had ... whatever Scott had. He wasn't home much, so I really didn't know what he did or whom he associated with, and I didn't care. Still don't."

"That's ... kind of sad," Christine said.

"It wasn't, and it's not. I was fulfilled, and Scott ... I'm sure that he was as well, because in the time I spent married to him, he never failed to do exactly what he wanted to do, when he wanted to do it."

"So there's no one that sticks out?" Christine said. "No one you can think of who might have held on to a grudge this long?"

"No," Janis said, "not from the time we were married. As I said, we barely interacted. We ate separately, we had separate bedrooms, different schedules. He woke after noon each day and stayed out until the wee hours, and I had a baby."

"Been there," Christine said. "I know what your schedule was like."

Janis nodded, smiling. "We saw each other once or twice a day, and we barely spoke. For the last seven years of our marriage."

"By the way," Christine said, taking advantage of the

opening Janis had provided, "Brian told me about what happened to your son. I'm very sorry. I can't imagine the pain."

"No," Janis said. "You can't." Silence stretched for several seconds as Janis stared at the table in front of her, and Christine started to wonder if she'd made a tactical error in bringing that up and lost Janis for good.

Thus far, Christine had been pleased to find that Janis wasn't the shivering wounded bird she'd been half-expecting to see. Perhaps Brian had overstated his wife's condition, or her medication was currently flush, but either way, Janis had appeared strong and confident to Christine … up until this moment, when Christine had taken an ill-advised risk and mentioned her son's death. She needed to change the subject and bring Janis back to the present.

"Mmm," Christine said. "This coffee is so good." Indeed, she'd forgotten that coffee this good even existed. There was no way she could ever replicate this beverage with her Keurig.

Janis snapped out of it, looked up, and said, "There was one fellow, Charlie Hawkins. A business partner, from well after we were married."

"I've talked to him, yes."

"And there were some … tawdry … rumors …"

"About the underage girl?" Christine said.

"Yes. So you know."

"I do. Both of those guys have alibis. One of them is strong, but the other is a little shaky, and I plan to look into it later today."

"I'm afraid, then," Janis said, "that I don't have much else to offer."

"Janis," Christine said. "I don't know how to ask this, other than to just ask it, and I hope you don't take this the wrong way. I've heard that you and Scott were at each other's throats for a while, after your divorce."

"*During* the divorce, actually, and for a while afterwards. It was a situation brought on by our attorneys, if you want the truth. There was no real acrimony between us other than that caused by unreasonable demands from both sides. And the repercussions from that dragged on for years, but eventually we did get over it. We even managed to develop a friendship of sorts, from a distance. But if you're asking, as I believe you are, whether I had reason to wish Scott dead, the answer is no. As I said earlier, I cared little whether he lived or died. I do believe the world might be a better place without Scott traipsing around leaving ruined lives behind him, but I could never have been part of a scheme to end his."

Christine was skeptical. Janis harbored no resentment of this guy whatsoever? After what she'd been through with him? And Christine thought the answer itself had sounded a little too pat and rehearsed. She was about to ask a follow-up question when Janis gasped and pointed at the clock on the wall.

"Oh my gosh," she said, "look at the time! I'm sorry, Christine, I hate to cut this short, but I've got to go." Her chair scraped across the floor as she backed up to stand.

"Oh, so soon? I feel like we were just getting started."

"I know, and it's been lovely, but I've an appointment across town in a few minutes that I can't miss."

"Well, all right," Christine said. "I appreciate you agreeing to talk to me, and I hope you find healing."

"Thank you. Before I go ..." She rummaged in a canvas shopping bag leaning against her chair leg. "I have something for you." She drew out a copy of *Pie to Die For* and handed it to Christine. "I know you didn't get a chance to pick one up the other night."

"Oh, thank you! How much?"

"It's a gift. I signed it for you, too. I hope you enjoy it."

"Thank you, Janis. That's very nice of you. And thank you again, for seeing me. I know it's been uncomfortable."

"Not at all. I wanted to do it. I hope you find the real killer, and it was very nice meeting you."

Christine laughed. "Wanna do it again next week?"

"Sure!" They both laughed, each knowing they would not be doing this ever again. Christine watched as Janis picked up her cup, still almost half full of vanilla latte, carried it to the trash can, and dropped it in. Then, with a final smile and a waggle of her fingers, she strode out the back door, leaving Christine sitting at the table alone.

She finished her own coffee as her thoughts swirled. Although she had started off liking the woman, she now couldn't escape the feeling that Janis had been lying to her, not only in the answer to her final question, but possibly before that as well. It wasn't anything Christine could put a finger on specifically, just a gut feeling that Janis had been trying too hard, as if she had something to hide. Right down to her sudden departure and the gifting of the book, which now struck Christine as a ploy designed to win her over and deflect suspicion. And a crude ploy, at that. Almost insulting.

Christine was also troubled by the fact she hadn't been able to ask about the money problems Brian had mentioned, and she hadn't had time to steer the conversation into that arena so that Janis might open it up herself.

Maybe she'd misread the entire situation. Maybe Janis was just socially awkward, and had been trying, albeit failing, to connect with Christine on a personal level while answering her questions as honestly as possible. Maybe Janis found her past difficult to talk about, so she sugar-coated her relationship with Scott as a matter of habit.

But Christine's instincts told her Janis was being disingenuous. And that could mean either she was somehow involved in Scott's murder, or, at least, she knew something about it that she wasn't saying.

She left String Theory with more questions than answers.

CHAPTER EIGHTEEN

AS PREDICTED, THE boys were still in bed, leaving Christine a little more time to get a couple of things done.

But she found herself in a quandary. She'd uncovered no material evidence in her interview of Janis O'Riordan, hadn't caught her in any outright lies. She couldn't exactly go to Ronnie Gaines now and say, "Hey, I talked to Janis and I'm pretty sure she was lying to me. I'm not sure how or why or even what about, but she must be guilty of *something* or she wouldn't lie, so don't you think you should drop the charges on Megan?"

That would get her laughed out of the room. She needed something more concrete, but she sensed she had seen the last of Janis O'Riordan and heard as much of Janis' side of the story as she was ever going to hear. That door had closed, and no amount of bashing her head against the wall would reopen it.

But that didn't mean Christine would forget about it. Janis' behavior meant something. It was part of the big picture, and it was up to Christine to figure out how it all fit together.

For the time being, though, she put it out of her mind. It

was time to pivot and attack the problem from a different angle.

Such as establishing the timeline of Randy Frey, who was still not off the hook.

She called Lisa.

"Hey," she said. "Can you check on somebody's tab from Saturday night for me?" Christine knew Lisa was the only one who could access the data she needed, and she also knew Lisa could do it from her phone, so there was no need to wait until they were both at the brewery.

"Absolutely," Lisa said. "I talked to Megan and I know what you're up to. I'll help in any way I can. What do you need to know?"

"Randy Frey. What time did he buy his last beer?"

"You think he might've done it?"

"Last night I did, but since then, I heard that he left before the murder happened. Just trying to verify that so I can rule him out."

"He bought his first and last beer at four-twenty-eight."

"Okay. It's still not a hundred percent exculpatory, but it helps. Thanks, Lisa."

"No problem. I can compile a list of people who bought beer both before and after the murder; would that help?"

"Yeah, that's a great idea. I wish I'd talked to you sooner." Truly, she did. Lisa, their resident IT guru, was an asset of which she should have availed herself earlier, but it hadn't been necessary. She'd been focused on one suspect at a time: first Keith Bonham, then Jerry McKernan, then Michael, then Brian Harrison, Tina Cornell, and Charlie Hawkins, and eliminated each one in order before her visit with Janis O'Riordan. There'd been no need for a list or a database, but now, with all the most likely suspects ruled out, they were down to the *unlikely* suspects, of which there were a veritable multitude. Maybe now was the time for that database.

"Consider it done," Lisa said. "It might take me a while, but I'll let you know when it's ready. We can figure this out ourselves, even if we have to print out the list and mark off names with a Sharpie until there's only one left."

Christine laughed. "I hope it doesn't come to that."

"Anything else I can do for you right now?"

Christine wanted to tell her that she hadn't yet ruled out Mark, but she didn't have the heart. "Not at the moment. I'll keep you posted."

Next, she needed to verify Randy Frey's alibi. She checked the schedule of the Aberdeen Ironbirds, the Single-A farm team for the Orioles. They had indeed played a game at home on Saturday night, against the Brooklyn Cyclones. So that part, at least, was true. Aberdeen was twenty-five minutes away from Forest Hill, and the game had started at six-thirty-five, so it was entirely reasonable that Randy Frey might leave around five o'clock to go home, grab some eats, maybe change clothes or meet up with whomever was going with him, and go to the game. That part of the story checked out.

Then she went back to Randy's Facebook page to see if he'd posted anything about going to that game.

Yep. Including selfies. One photo of Randy and two other smiling men had the scoreboard in the background, and it showed that the game had yet to start.

Christine figured it was barely possible that Randy could have come back to the Groove at five-forty, murdered Scott Cornell, dragged the body around the corner, slipped out the back door, hidden the weapon, made his way on foot to wherever he'd left his car, driven to Ripken Stadium, parked, waited in the queue to get inside, and taken a selfie before first pitch. Barely.

But not bloody likely.

Randy was either the cleverest murderer since Hannibal Lecter, or he was off the hook.

Christine sighed in frustration. *Wrong again.*

Regarding the person who had actually swung the bulldog pipe, she'd systematically eliminated every suspect on her list, with the exception of the one person she refused to consider: Mark Moody, her boss and friend.

She was missing something. Maybe she'd been too exclusive in formulating her list of suspects. Maybe she needed to branch out.

Perhaps she needed to circle back to those scenarios that involved murder-for-hire, which would reopen the cases on Brian, Janis, and Tina. Especially Janis, who'd been cagey with her. Or perhaps she needed to reconsider the idea that someone may have thought they were killing Mark, opening up a whole new list of suspects.

To widen the net even further: What if Scott had merely been collateral damage in someone's quest to besmirch the reputation of Double Groove? Or that of Janis O'Riordan? What if the *identity* of the victim was inconsequential, as long as the crime happened where and when it did?

She shook her head. Such a scenario would open up as a suspect every last person who had been at Double Groove that night, and some who hadn't. Literally anyone could have snuck into the back door without ever showing their face inside. To narrow that down would be an almost impossible undertaking.

She needed to know the motive. That would simplify things.

She began to despair. For Megan's sake, she would not, *could* not give up, but she had no idea what the next step might be. She was floundering, and she knew it.

Maybe she needed to stop thinking about it. Sometimes when she couldn't find something, say her wallet or the TV remote, and she forced herself to stop looking for it, sometimes it would appear on its own as if by magic. Maybe this was one of those times.

She turned her attention to a problem she knew she could do something about. The truck.

She dialed the number Strazz had sent her.

"'Lo!"

"Is this Julius?"

"Ayup. Who's this?"

"My name's Christine. I got your number from a friend, and I'm interested in your '41 Truck if it's still available."

"Ayup."

"So … is it still available?"

"Ayup. Just said that."

"Would it be possible for me to come look at it sometime today?"

Silence.

"Are you still there?" Christine said.

"Hold your horses. I'm checkin'."

Christine kept her mouth shut.

"'Bout noon should work," he said. "Bring beer."

Christine almost burst out laughing. "Um … okay. What kind?"

"Beer. 'Merican. Nothin' fancy."

"Gotcha. See you then."

Holy crap, she thought as she hung up. *Some people*. But if cheap beer was the bribe it took to get that truck, then cheap beer it would be.

Bobby had already seen the truck. She was sure he wouldn't mind if she went to see it today without him.

She checked the time. She still had an hour before the local beer store opened up.

* * *

A bit later, the boys crawled out of bed, hungry and eager to face whatever another summer day might bring. Typically they ate cereal for breakfast, but on Mondays and Tuesdays, when Christine was off, they liked pancakes.

"Take it easy on the syrup," she said, once they were seated and tearing into the hot flapjacks.

"Okay," they both said with little conviction.

"There's leftovers in the fridge if you get hungry again. I'll be back in a half hour, though. Stay out of trouble if you can."

"Mm-hm," Kyle said.

Christine knew they'd heard her, but whether they'd processed what she said was up in the air. She shrugged and walked out the door. *Boys.*

She drove with her windows open, reveling in the summer morning air, and parked at a small strip mall. As she entered the beer store, she tried to recall the last time she'd purchased cheap American beer. It had been in her early twenties, surely. Back before the days when she'd deprogrammed Bobby by dragging him to the bars in Fells Point, where she'd introduced him to pale ales, IPAs, stouts, porters, and wheat beers. And broken him away from the cheap American beers his German-Irish family had raised him to venerate.

Standing before the case, she let her eyes travel over the dizzying array of American beers. Which ones were currently under boycott for supposedly violating some basic tenet of 'Muricanism? She couldn't remember. She took a chance and grabbed a twelve-pack of Miller High Life in cans. Then she tamped down her embarrassment as she took the carton to the register and paid for it.

As she scurried back to her Highlander, eyes straight ahead so that she wouldn't notice if she was spotted, she reflected that there was no bottom, no indignity to which she would not subject herself if it furthered her goal of obtaining this truck. If she'd been asked to, she would have bought cheap American beer while naked.

Well, okay. Maybe there is a bottom.

But she would go to Julius' house, she would give him his beer, she would even drink one with him if that's what he wanted, and she would check out that truck. If it was at all drivable, she would offer him $10,000 less than what he was asking, and she would drive that truck home and put it in her garage with the '32. Later, she and Bobby would move the Shelby to the garage at his work for storage.

She went home to check on the boys and make sure the house hadn't burned down. She did a few household chores, checking the time every few minutes in anticipation of her date with Julius.

At eleven o'clock, her phone rang. It was Julius.

"Truck ain't for sale no more."

"What?" she said, every nerve jangling.

"Truck ain't for sale."

"Why not?"

"Sold."

"What? I mean how?"

"Fella come here, offered me money, I took it 'n' give 'im the keys. He drove it away."

"But I bought you beer!"

"Can still bring it, if y'wanna."

One of the worst things about cellphones was that you couldn't slam them down to hang up. She settled for pushing on the "End" button *really hard* while snarling, "Arrgh!"

She felt tears coming. This day had been nothing but a series of setbacks since she woke up. And now this, the topper, just when she'd thought there was nothing else that could go wrong.

She blamed Bobby. If he'd let her go look at the truck last night, instead of trotting out lame excuse after lame excuse ... *I told him*, she thought. *I told him it would be gone.*

But oh, no. Trust him, he said. Trust him. Tomorrow would be fine.

Oh, was he gonna get the cold shoulder tonight.

CHAPTER NINETEEN

FEELING HELPLESS AND lost, Christine bounced from room to room like a mouse in a maze, searching for another menial task to keep herself occupied. Nothing immediately came to the forefront.

She thought about taking the boys for an outing of some sort, maybe a park or a trail ride, but after having shopped themselves out with Mom the day before, they wanted nothing to do with her today. They had their own plots and designs for the day, and those did not involve Mom.

It was not even noon yet. An entire day loomed before Christine, with all her plans having unraveled and no clear road before her. She had no idea if the sky was yellow or the sun was blue.

She felt herself slipping into a tailspin. Frustration, helplessness, anger, and betrayal all clashed for control of her soul, and the result was a complete gridlock.

Maybe this amateur sleuth thing was just not her gig, after all. Maybe it was time to give up and let the pros handle it.

I tried, Megan, she thought. *I tried*.

She wandered into the living room and sat on the couch,

not even bothering to flick on the TV, and tried unsuccessfully to think about nothing. Maybe a nap ...

*　*　*

It could've been minutes, it could've been hours. She had no idea how long she'd slouched there, pinned down by lethargy and apathy, when her sons rescued her by entering the room and announcing they were going to Jimmy's to hang out for the day. She checked the wall clock and found she'd only been asleep for a half hour. She nodded her assent, watched the boys bustle out the door, and somehow gathered herself to overcome inertia and rise. On some reptilian level she recognized the chance to pursue a measure of mental and emotional recovery. And for her, that always involved driving. Preferably in a classic car.

She went to the garage, slipped behind the wheel of the '32 Coupe, and raised the garage door. Just the act of turning the key and hearing the engine roar to life was cathartic and made Christine smile.

Minutes later, with Christine at the wheel, the Coupe rumbled along Maryland Route 24, winding its way down into the pastoral valley carved over the eons by Deer Creek. The coupe's black lacquer finish gleamed in the sun; its well-tuned engine ran with a pleasant rumble, and blatted a gratifying roar each time she downshifted for a tight curve. The smells of ripe peaches and fresh mown grass tickled her nose and brought another smile to her lips. The tires hummed on the blacktop, her blonde hair tossed in the wind from the open windows, and she imagined she could feel the negative vibes being purged from her pores as newer, more constructive ones stole in via her wide-open senses.

As she continued northward, she reflected that there may have been a genetic component to her chosen approach to self-therapy. Her father, a gearhead like her, had once raced VW bugs on dirt tracks. For fun. For therapy. And now she continued the tradition. *Hell, if it ain't broke, don't fix it.*

She entered Rocks State Park, the trees on either side of the road meeting overhead to form a tunnel of dappled shade, and tooled along, with the alternating wide flats and rushing cataracts of rock-strewn Deer Creek to her right. She passed the stone bridge abutment from the old Ma & Pa Railroad, still standing after the railway's closure some seventy years ago, downshifted, and drifted into the first creekside pulloff. The tires crackled over loose gravel as she joined one other vehicle, a battered old Jeep Cherokee, in the unpaved lot, and parked the Coupe facing the creek.

From the driver's seat she could now sit and watch the water slide gently over its bed of sandstone gravel and mud, listen to the birds, and reboot her brain.

It was a place she had sought out countless times in the past when her mind needed clearing. Although she hadn't done so for many years, this spot remained sacred to her. The place hadn't changed a bit in the two decades since she'd first seen it, and that constancy alone gave her comfort. She took a deep breath, held it for half a second, and released it in a gust. A grin, unbidden, spread across her face.

A flicker of motion at her ten o'clock caught her eye, and she turned her head to see a great blue heron high-stepping through the shallows. She watched it for a while as it marched along at its own stately pace, occasionally stabbing its sharp beak into the water for a minnow or a crayfish.

Without warning, the heron sprang into the air. Christine

held her breath as it followed the creek bed downstream, soaring from left to right at her eye level, and finally disappearing as the undergrowth and boles of trees increasingly obscured her view of its path. She was amazed at its majestic wingspan, but disappointed by its departure.

Back to her left, another animal came into view, this one of the two-legged variety. A fisherman dressed in hip waders, a tan multi-pocketed vest, and a camo-print ball cap moved, one slow laborious step at a time, downstream toward her. It occurred to her that he had more than likely been the reason the heron had taken wing.

The fisherman stopped and drew back his right arm, then flung it forward. A bright green ribbon-like line shot out from the tip of the rod, and the fisherman drew his arm back again. The line came back over his head. The fisherman threw it forward again, and back again, and forward again, and Christine watched the sinuous motion of the line as it grew longer and longer in the air with each toss. At last, he released it, and the entire length of fluorescent green plastic, thick as yarn, settled on the surface of the water, generally stretching away from the fisherman, but forming a looping, undulating pattern on the water that was pleasing to her eye.

The fisherman waited. *How are the fish not gonna see that line?* Christine asked herself.

She had little experience with fishing, and zero with fly fishing. As a child, her father had raised her on dipsticks and spark plugs, not tap shoes and tutus, and certainly not on rods and reels. On one occasion, a childhood friend's family had invited her to go along with them on a fishing trip to a local pond, and she had learned, to some extent, how to cast a lure. But it had been nothing like this. This was ... fascinating. Almost hypnotic.

After half a minute or so, the fisherman reeled his line

back in and took a few more careful steps downstream. Then he repeated the whole casting ritual.

Christine watched as he continued in his progress downstream, three steps, a cast, wait, two steps, another cast, wait, five steps, another cast, another waiting period.

She couldn't look away.

At last, the fisherman drew abreast of the parking area and reeled in his line. He climbed the bank, hip waders gleaming as they sloughed off water, and walked to the old Cherokee parked ten yards or so to her left. He opened the Jeep's hatch and slid his fly rod within. As he began undoing the buckles on his waders, he glanced toward Christine and caught her staring.

"Hi!" he said, smiling.

"Hello," she replied.

"Nice wheels ya got there."

"Thanks. Any luck?"

"Oh, not much." He patted the creel that hung on him like a fanny pack. "Got two smallmouth in here. Too late in the year for trout, but I can't not fish. Every so often I just gotta get out'n the woods, ya know?"

"Yup. Know the feeling." As the man removed his cap and tossed it into the Jeep, she saw that he bore a striking resemblance to actor Andy Griffith. Not the younger Mayberry version, but the Ben Matlock silver fox version. Minus the grey suit, of course. The man had to be in his mid- to late seventies, and he was still out here, wading in creeks, experiencing life. A part of her was proud of him. A less condescending part of her wanted to *be* him.

"Can I see the fish?" she asked.

The fisherman chuckled. "Sure. I ain't gonna say no to a purty girl in a hot car. Don't tell my wife I said that," he added with a wink.

As she climbed out of the Coupe, she said, smiling,

"Your secret's safe with me."

She and the fisherman were alone, surrounded by miles of rural landscape devoid of human witnesses other than the ones passing by on the road, and those were in moving cars, eyes focused forward. Yet, despite the fact he had already flirted with her, she felt no sense of alarm. It wasn't anything she could put a finger on, but she knew to the center of her being that this was a friendly, gentle old man who posed no threat to her.

Besides, she was pretty sure she could take him, if it came to that.

"What year is that?" he asked as she approached.

"Thirty-two."

"Before I was born. My buddy Jim had a thirty-four, though, back in the sixties. Didn't look near as spiffy as yours. Still had the fenders on it. Boy, we beat the hell outta that old girl," he said with a laugh, showing all his teeth except the one lateral incisor that was missing. "Drove 'er till the wheels fell off. Boy, you're a long drink o' water, aintcha?"

As they drew near each other, Christine could see they were on eye level with each other, a not uncommon occurrence in her life. She smiled. "So I've heard. I'm Christine," she said, extending her hand.

He took her hand in his big gnarly paw. She felt calluses accumulated through years of manual labor, and the strength to grind her knuckles into dust if he were so inclined, but he applied only moderate pressure. "Name's Marlin," he said. "Good to meetcha."

"Like Marlon Brando?"

"No, Mar-lin, like the fish."

"Gotcha. Nice to meet you as well," she said.

"I used to say Marlin like Marlin Perkins, but nobody knows who the hell he was anymore."

Christine smiled. She indeed had no idea who Marlin Perkins had been, but she wasn't ready to admit it to this gentleman.

Marlin opened the lid on his creel and waved her closer. Two small greenish-brown fish, each less than eight inches in length, rested within. "Ain't much to take home," he said with another chuckle. "Once I fry 'em up, be about enough for a sammitch. Usually I don't take nothin', I throw 'em all back. Just had me a hankerin' for a fish sammitch today. That there's some goooood eatin'."

Christine laughed. In addition to *looking* like Andy Griffith, Marlin's homespun mode of speech also sounded like him. "Whadja catch 'em with?" she said, catching herself subconsciously imitating him.

"Welllll, I tried me a few things, but I finally settled on a little ol' popper. That's what I got these two buggers on."

"No, I meant ... your rod, the line, the whole mess."

"Oh, oh, oh!" he said, face alight. "You never seen a fly rod before?"

"Not in real life."

"Well, lemme show ya." He retrieved the fly rod from the Jeep. "Wanna learn?"

"Learn what?"

"How to cast."

"What, right here?" she said.

"Sure, why not? Gotta start somewhere. We'll just move over here to the center of the lot, where there ain't no tree branches to get hung up in."

She followed him a few feet away from the vehicles, thinking, *What am I doing?*

"What brings ya out here today, anyway?" Marlin asked.

"Rebooting."

Marlin nodded his head. "This here's the best way there is to reboot. Take my word for it."

"Thanks, but really, I'm too old to learn to fly fish."

"Why, how old are ya?"

"Forty-one."

Marlin's eyes crinkled when he laughed. "Shucks, you ain't old, kid. I was older'n you when I started. I been at it for thirty-some year now, and I'm still learnin', but you got thirty-some year ahead o' ya, doncha figger?"

"I hope so."

"Now listen at me: The best time to plant a tree is twenty year ago."

Christine laughed. "I guess that's true, but—"

"Ya know when the second-best time is?" His warm brown eyes stared holes in her.

Christine shook her head.

"Today," he said. "The second-best time is today. Now ya wanna try this or not?"

Christine couldn't help but laugh at Marlin's cheerful enthusiasm as she took the rod from his hands. "You do this all the time?" she asked. "Teach random people how to fly fish?"

Marlin chuckled again. "Not all the time. But you ain't the first, and ya prolly won't be the last. I guess I'm sorta whatcha call the elder statesman of Deer Creek. I ain't like a lotta these idjits out here, hoardin' all their secrets like they was gold. I love what I do, and I enjoy passin' it around. Now listen at me…"

First, he taught her the names of all the parts of the fly tackle. The rod, the reel, the fly line, the leader, the tippet, and the fly itself.

"Why do you have so many flies?" she asked when he showed her a small pocket box full of the colorful intricate lures.

"Well, first off," he said with a laugh, "I lose a lot of 'em. In trees, on underwater rocks and branches, and in fish that break the leader. It's part of the game. Second, ya gotta have different flies for different times of year, different fish, different rivers. It's called followin' the hatch. Whatever nymphs are hatchin' at the time, that's what the fish are lookin' for, so you try to imitate 'em."

"Where do you get these?"

"I tie 'em m'self."

"You're kidding. Would I have to learn that too?"

"Not right away. I'll give ya some, and I can tell ya what stores to go to where ya can buy 'em already made. There's a lot to fly fishin', a lotta skill and a lotta knowledge, but we can talk about all that stuff later. Today I just wanna learn you how to flang this here thing and have it land where ya want it to go. Now hold it in your right hand like this … you right-handed?"

"Yes."

"Okay, hold it like I showed ya, and start by strippin' some line off the reel. Just drop it on the ground, that's right. Now flang it."

Her first cast was a disaster. Her second, a little less so. Marlin gave her good-natured answers to her occasional questions. He was gentle with her mistakes and his self-deprecating humor put her at ease.

The next hour and a half passed by in what seemed to her like about fifteen or twenty minutes, and by the end of that time he'd coached her to the point where she could hit a small area the size of a garbage can lid, about half the time.

"I think that's enough for today," he said. "That arm must be plumb tuckered by now. I wantcha to take that rod home with ya and practice in your yard."

"What? Oh, no, I couldn't."

He nodded vigorously. "I got seven of 'em. Take it, and I'm gonna give ya my number. Call me if ya have any questions, and meet me here next week. If ya decide it ain't for you, ya can gimme that rod back then."

"Marlin, I ... I don't know how to thank you."

"You can thank me by learnin' the art. I got a feelin' about you. I think you're fly-fishin' material."

"I appreciate that. I'll give it a try. And this couldn't have come at a better time, believe me. I've had a hell of a day so far."

"You wanna tell me about it?"

"Let's just say I'm looking for something. A couple of somethings, actually. And today, every time I thought I was getting closer to one of them, it turned out to be a dead end. Now it feels like my whole plan is kind of circling the drain."

Marlin nodded, frowning. "Had days like that, bet your bottom dollar. Now listen at me, missy. Sometimes the fish you're tryin' for ain't really the fish you want, but ya don't know it yet. Sometimes ya go ahead 'n' give up on that bugger, and ya move downstream a little and cast at a different hole, and along comes another'n outa nowhere and takes that fly, and ya realize he was the bugger ya shoulda been castin' at all along. And ya start to get sorta whatcha call an instinct. Sometimes it's about patience 'n' persistence, and sometimes it's about knowin' when it's time to give up 'n' move on. And *all* the time ... *all* the time, missy ... it's about knowin' which time is which. Seems to me like ya might have that figgered out already, or ya wouldn't be here, wouldja?"

CHAPTER TWENTY

CHRISTINE WENT HOME and spent the next two hours in her back yard, practicing what Marlin had taught her. And thinking.

At the end of that time, her arm truly was "plumb tuckered." She hung the fly rod on some bicycle hooks in the shed and went inside to start something for dinner. The boys came home, and Bobby followed soon afterward.

Dinner was quiet. After eating, the boys went to their rooms to do their respective things, and Bobby sat in the living room in front of the TV.

Christine seethed. Her mood had improved considerably since noon, but she was still unhappy with her husband and had said virtually nothing to him since he walked in the door.

And yet, he seemed to be oblivious to the sullen waves of resentment that she imagined she radiated. Of course, her taciturn silence had left him with no way to know that, because of his procrastination, the best truck they had yet found had been sold to someone else. But still, it rankled her that he had somehow failed to pick up on her mood and ask her about it, failed to make the mistake that would have given her what she so needed: the opportunity to pounce.

Frustrated, Christine announced that she was tired, and wanted to get some sleep, since tomorrow she had to go back to work, and went to bed without so much as a goodnight kiss.

* * *

When she arrived at Double Groove the next morning, she was pleased to find co-owner Kyle Waters' Ducati 350 Scrambler parked out back. She and Kyle shared an appreciation for classic machines, the difference in the number of wheels notwithstanding, and she always enjoyed brewing with him as well.

"Hey," she said as she slipped in through the back door. "Brought the bike out today, huh?"

"Yeah," Kyle said, "the forecast looks good. No rain in it for the next three days. How you been?"

Christine gave him a basic rundown of the last two days, and they talked a little about the night of the murder itself, since Kyle had missed it.

"Where's Lisa, anyway?" Christine asked. "Isn't she supposed to be here today?"

"Mark called this morning. She's got some kind of stomach bug."

"Uh-oh. Hope he doesn't get it, too. We'd be down to just you, me, Steven, and Michael. So what's the plan today?"

"We were gonna brew some Dirty White IPA today," Kyle said, "but we're short on Simcoe hops. I don't have time to run out to another brewer to borrow some, so how about we start some Helles Bells instead?"

"Works for me."

Within five minutes, they were fully immersed in their work, and Christine took comfort in rote tasks and physical labor. Kyle being a quiet guy, they didn't talk much as they worked, and Christine spent much of that time going over unlikely scenarios and trying to decide on the next step in her quest to exonerate Megan.

Three hours passed before they got a break. By that time, Christine's right arm was sore as hell, but it was only the ache of muscle building, not debilitating, and in fact almost pleasant. Her ankle injury, on the other hand, was long forgotten.

And she was still at an impasse as far as the murder case.

With cleanup behind them and the taproom now open, Christine and Kyle moved out to see what business was like. It was early on a Wednesday, so they didn't expect much.

When the door to the taproom opened, they heard Blackberry Smoke spinning … a solid clue that Michael Reisinger was working the bar. And sure enough, they found him there. Alone.

"Where's Steven?" Kyle asked. With Megan on leave, Steven had volunteered to take her shifts this week.

"I dunno," Michael said. "Haven't seen him. It's been okay, though, not much business."

"I can see that," Kyle said, "but it's weird he's not here. I didn't hear anything from him either." Kyle, being one third of the ownership triumvirate and the only one on duty that day, should have been the first to know if anyone had called out.

"He's probably just running late," Christine said. "I can help out for a while until he gets here."

Kyle went back to the brewhouse while Christine and Michael shared the bar. "I hope he's okay," Christine said.

"Yeah," Michael said. "It *is* weird for him not to show

and not to even say anything."

One of the five patrons in the taproom was Ronnie Gaines, and he waved Christine over to the end of the B-side bar, where he and Sheriff Alan Curtis customarily sat.

"Hey," he said as Christine approached him. "Sorry if I came on too hard the other day. I hope you understand."

"I do," Christine said. "I know you have a job to do. And I don't think you'll have to worry about me meddling anymore. I'm about to give up. I'm not getting anywhere."

"We're not either, to be honest. CI has Scott's laptop, which is usually a treasure trove, but I heard Kingery tell George yesterday the only thing they got out of it was that Scott liked *Murder, She Wrote*."

Christine burst out laughing. "You're kidding. How could they tell?"

"Internet history, I suppose. He even seemed to have a favorite episode that he watched multiple times recently. Season Seven, Episode Five. Can you believe that?"

They shared a laugh together, and the tension between them drained away. "Need another?" Christine asked.

"Sure. Bang Your Hops, please."

"Gotcha."

As she poured Ronnie's beer, Michael sidled up to her and said, "I just tried to call Steven. He's not answering his phone."

"You leave a message?"

"Yeah. But I'm starting to worry."

"Me too," she said. "Hey, how was the Billy Strings show the other night?"

Michael's face lit up. "Aw, man, it was awesome. Wanna see some videos?"

"Sure! What you got?"

Michael showed her three videos he'd taken on his phone from different songs.

"Really talented guy," she said.

"He's incredible, and so was the light show. It was like a Pink Floyd show, only with bluegrass."

Michael: officially and permanently ruled out.

* * *

Six o'clock. The deck outside was filling up, and several more patrons were drinking in the taproom as well. Steven had yet to show up or call back, and Christine's back was starting to hurt from standing, when Mark arrived.

"Go on home," Mark said. "Mike and I can handle it."

"I'm worried sick about Steven."

"He'll turn up."

Christine nodded, but privately, she wondered. Steven had picked the worst possible time to go dark like this, and a couple of chilling possibilities had taken root in her mind. One, that the murderer had struck again, taking Steven for reasons unknown. And two, that Steven *was* the murderer. She reviewed in her mind the evidence that had been uncovered regarding Steven's guilt or innocence.

He'd been standing right beside her the entire twenty minutes that were in question. Hadn't he?

A sick feeling crept over her. She remembered an evening not long ago when Steven had done a magic show at Double Groove, and she, along with seventy-five other people, had been a hundred percent certain that Kyle was inside a black curtain that Steven held suspended from a metal hoop. They'd all seen Kyle standing there when Steven raised the curtain around him. But when Steven dropped the hoop and the curtain fell, Kyle was gone. And seconds later, Kyle had come trotting out from the brewhouse. In heels and a blue flapper dress. Shock, awe.

Steven was a master of illusion. But just exactly how

talented was he? Could he make himself appear to be somewhere that he wasn't? More specifically, could he create the illusion that he was behind the bar with Christine, when he was actually in the brewhouse killing his ex-uncle for spoiling his card trick?

Crazy, Christine thought. *You're losing your mind, girl.*

But again ... she was down to the unlikely suspects at this point. And, come to think of it, *why* had Steven tried so hard to deflect suspicion onto Michael the last time she'd seen him?

She left Double Groove with the mystery of Steven's whereabouts still unresolved.

*　*　*

Bobby had prepared dinner ... a sure sign that he wanted to mend fences. Which was strange, considering she hadn't told him any fences were down, at least overtly. But a part of her was gratified to know that her message last night had, after all, penetrated his troglodytic skull.

Regardless of the reason for it, she thanked him and they ate. It would have been nice if she could have thrown him a bone and opened up about what had been bothering her since last night, but she was distracted.

"What's on your mind?" he asked.

"Oh, it's just ... well, Steven's missing." *Season Seven, Episode Five*, she thought, apropos of nothing.

"Whaddya mean, missing?" he said sharply.

"I mean he didn't show up at work, and he doesn't answer his phone."

"That's not normal, is it?"

"Not even a little bit," she said.

"No wonder you're so preoccupied."

"Do you know what streaming platform carries *Murder,*

She Wrote?"

Bobby shook his head like a dog clearing its ears. "What? No. I mean, who cares?"

"I do." She did some searching on her phone. "Here it is. Peacock. Prime. And Pluto. The three P's, how about that?"

"Wow, that's great. Now we can watch *Murder, She Wrote* twenty-four/seven."

"I just want to see one episode. Season Seven, Episode Five." She got up to put her plate and silver in the dishwasher.

"Why?"

"It came up at work today. Wanna watch it with me? Come on, it'll be fun."

"Be still, my heart." Bobby shrugged and got up to follow her to the living room. Men would take *anything* offered as an olive branch, even a forty-year-old episode of a cheesy TV mystery series starring a washed-up Hollywood actress in the twilight of her career. Christine almost laughed aloud.

They settled on the couch. Christine commandeered the remote and navigated her way through Pluto's less-than-user-friendly menu system, until she found the proper season and episode of *Murder, She Wrote*.

After sitting through the opening theme, with its oddly jarring juxtaposition of piano music, typewriter keys striking, and car crashes, they watched the show until the first commercial break, about fifteen minutes into the episode.

Christine spoke up. "Can we pause this for a minute? I need to go check something."

"Right now?"

"Yeah. I think I might have figured out why she was being so cagey."

"Who?"

"Janis O'Riordan."

She left her baffled husband on the couch and ran to her nightstand, where she'd dropped her Janis O'Riordan titles Saturday night after finally being allowed to come home. She slid Janis' last *New York Times* Bestseller, a novel called *Death of the Blues* that Christine had quite enjoyed, from the middle of the stack. She opened it to the first chapter, skimmed a few pages. Then she skipped ahead to Chapter 2 and skimmed a few more.

She closed the book with a thump and took it with her back to the living room, where she sat back down next to Bobby. "I read this book last year," she said. "It takes place in New Orleans."

"Hey, just like this show," he said.

"Yeah. In Chapter 1, a famous blues musician dies, and a few days later, a member of his band is discovered strangled."

Bobby's eyebrows shot up. "Huh."

"Right? Exactly like this show so far. The names are different, but the plot is the same. Let's watch the rest." She picked up the remote and pushed Play.

By the midway point of the show, Christine knew. But she kept watching, despite the fact that she knew how the episode would end. Or at least she thought she did.

She was right. The show ended, and it could not have been more clear.

The sheer audacity of it took Christine's breath away. *How did she think she would get away with it? How did no one on Goodreads or Amazon ever figure this out?*

It was so blatant. This was more than a simple reimagining. It was deeper than that, down to ridiculous details, like the fact that the murder stemmed from a romantic relationship that the bluesman had had twenty years before, with a woman who ended up murdered after they broke up. Down to the fact that it was the bluesman's son who had committed both murders, twenty years apart.

Christine almost couldn't believe it, but there was no way around it: Janis O'Riordan had ripped off the plot of her last book from an old episode of *Murder, She Wrote*. She had changed the year and the names of the characters, no more, and that was probably only in hopes of avoiding detection by search engines. Everything else was exactly the same.

And to think there was a time that I was almost starstruck with her, Christine thought. It was mortifying.

Janis had plagiarized her last novel, and if she did that once … who knew how many more of her novels were recycled stories from old TV shows?

And Scott Cornell had found out about it. The cops had found that very episode of *Murder, She Wrote* in his Internet history, multiple times. Scott Cornell, who was, among other things, a compulsive gambler, and who had in the past resorted to crime to pay off his debts. Christine doubted he would find it beneath himself to do so again, even if his ex-wife were the victim.

And another data point: Janis had been worried about money lately, to her husband's bewilderment.

It all fit.

Scott Cornell had been blackmailing Janis O'Riordan.

Bingo. Motive.

CHAPTER TWENTY-ONE

NOW THE QUESTION was *Who would want to kill Scott Cornell to keep him from blackmailing Janis, or exposing her fraud?* The obvious suspects were Janis herself and her husband, Brian Harrison. Janis clearly could not have done it herself, and most likely neither could Brian. Christine had plans to verify his alibi, but be that as it may ... could either or both of them have hired someone else to do the deed? Up until a few minutes ago, she had doubted that as well, but with blackmail in the mix, who knew?

And besides those two, were there any others? Who else would care enough about Janis O'Riordan's reputation to be willing to kill to protect her? Should Christine be casting a wider net?

Off the top of her head, Christine couldn't think of many who fit the bill. Janis had no living children or parents. She had one sister, Steven's mother. Could she have done it? What about Steven himself? Could that be why he'd disappeared? Was he onto the fact that Christine was getting close?

No. That didn't make sense. Steven had never expressed any type of devotion to his aunt, and had in fact stated the opposite.

But could that have been intentional, a smokescreen? Doth Steven protest too much?

What about close friends of Janis? Or her agent? Christine would have to speak to Janis again to go down that particular rabbit hole. And that didn't seem likely.

Never mind. First order of business was to find out, once and for all, whether Brian had been on the deck at the time of the murder. The cops had it as a given, but Christine had yet to prove it to her own satisfaction. And the ones to talk to about it were the Willigs, Jeff and Amy. Jeff, because he was a musician and may have even known Brian from String Theory, and because he'd been out on the deck, not yet performing, but waiting for the indoor festivities to end. And Amy, because she wandered a lot and took a lot of pictures.

If either of them was able to attest to the fact that Brian *was* on the deck from five-forty to six-ten, then the next thing to look into would be murder-for-hire. Christine didn't think she had the capability to do that. She'd have to tell Ronnie what she'd learned, let the Sheriff's Office handle it, and hope for the best.

But meanwhile: Jeff and Amy. Checking the time, she realized it was after nine o'clock. She felt uncomfortable calling them at this hour, so she shot Jeff a text.

> **Christine:** You guys up for a short phone call?

She waited a few seconds, but got no reply.
Damn.
Seventeen minutes later, as she and Bobby searched for something else to watch to take them to bedtime, Jeff's text came in.

Jeff: Kinda noisy here. We're at Alecraft for teacher's night.

Uh-oh. Alecraft, a very small brewery in downtown Bel Air, struggling to survive in a glutted market, offered twenty percent discount to teachers on alternate Wednesdays. Amy was a teacher and a beer-lover. There was no point trying to collar her for any kind of productive phone call.

Christine: Ok I wanted to talk to both of you abt Sat night. Meet me tomorrow at DG?

Jeff: What time?

Christine: I'll be there all day

Jeff: We can be there at 5

Christine: Thanks see you then

Christine put her phone down and watched the local news with Bobby. After a couple of segments, she glanced over at her husband and saw that he'd fallen asleep. She still felt a bit of lingering resentment toward him, but it was blurring with time.

She closed her eyes.

* * *

Thursday at Double Groove. Kyle had gone to a neighboring brewery after work yesterday to borrow some Simcoe hops, so Christine had a busy morning brewing Dirty White IPA with Mark, and then canning a batch of

Crossroads Cream Ale. Steven was still a no-show, and no one had heard from him, or his girlfriend either. Repeated phone calls to both numbers kept going to voicemail. At what point should they call the police? Christine feared that point may have already come and gone.

She frowned. There were three possibilities regarding Steven that she could think of. One, he was dead, killed by the murderer because he either a) had found out who did it, or b) had been in on the blackmailing. Two, he was the murderer himself, and had gone into hiding. Three, some other, legitimate reason none of them knew about.

Christine had also begun to worry about Tina Cornell. The possibility existed that Tina, being Scott's wife, had known about the blackmailing scheme and may have even assisted in it. She certainly would have profited from it. That said, might the killer now be targeting her next?

"Mark," she said as her boss walked past her, "should we be thinking about calling the cops?"

"About Steven?"

"Yeah."

"I don't know. When was the last time we saw him?"

"Sunday. But we were closed Monday and Tuesday, so he's technically only been missing since yesterday. I know it hasn't been long, but it's odd that he hasn't even called, and isn't answering his phone."

"Hmm. I'll talk to the sheriff about it. He should be in today."

"Okay. How's Lisa, by the way?"

"Not as sick as she was, but she's really weak. She was still in bed when I left."

"Did she have a chance to work on that database she and I talked about?"

Mark's face pinched in momentary concentration. "I don't know. She didn't say anything about it to me."

"Okay. Don't bother her about it. I know she'll do it when she's able." Until then, Christine still had other loose ends to tie up, such as whether Mark, Lisa, Steven, or Brian Harrison had opportunity to commit murder. Also, if she had time, she could look at pics to find out once and for all whether Charlie Hawkins had been at the party. But first, she'd have to find out what Charlie Hawkins looked like. She'd only spoken to him on the phone.

"You're probably next, by the way," she said to Mark. "To get sick, I mean."

Mark laughed. "I hope not. Lisa was miserable."

"Don't you dare bring it in here, whatever you do."

"Oh, Vike. You take the fun out of *everything.*"

After the busy morning, Christine had a hectic afternoon in the taproom and on the deck. She did find time to text Megan during a lull, and learned that she was at the Baltimore Zoo with her boyfriend and her ten-year-old son, Dominic. She was feeling fine, but she still wasn't ready to talk.

Christine couldn't say she blamed her.

Five o'clock rolled around. Pink Floyd on the turntable, Michael and Kyle behind the bar. A cast of regulars sat at the bar, including Alan Curtis and Ronnie Gaines. No Jeff and Amy, but a text came in from Jeff.

Jeff: Leaving now. See you in 20 min

Christine sighed. She'd been hoping to get home for dinner. Now that was out the window.

She saw Mark talking to the two men from the Sheriff's Office, and assumed the conversation would likely be about Steven.

At five-thirty-five, Jeff entered the taproom in a Double

Groove trucker hat, with Amy and her flowing red mane right behind him, and then it took them a while to get to the bar, with a dozen or so people knowing one or the other of them and wanting to exchange pleasantries.

"Hey," Christine said after finally serving them their beers. "Wanna meet me over there at that corner table? I kind of want to keep this on the DL."

"Sure," Jeff said, smiling through his goatee.

Christine followed the couple to the corner table. Heart's *Dog and Butterfly* was now playing.

"So, I was wondering," Christine began. "Jeff, you know Brian Harrison, right?"

"I recognized him from String Theory, yeah. I wouldn't say I know him."

"You remember he was on the deck Saturday night? During Janis' presentation?"

"Yeah, he was sitting with a couple of other guys I didn't know, right up in front near the band."

"Was he there the whole time? I mean, would you have noticed if he left for five minutes or so, just before six o'clock?"

Jeff cast his eyes to the ceiling, thinking back. "I mean, I probably wouldn't have noticed if he went to the food truck or something for a couple of minutes. I can't say for sure."

To the food truck, or around behind the building, Christine thought. Another question for the food truck that had been there, that she filed away for later.

"How about you, Amy?" she said. "Did you take any pictures out there around that time that would establish his presence on the deck?"

"I don't know," she said. "I did take some pictures on the deck, but I don't remember what time. Let's look." She withdrew her phone from her purse, and navigated to the

Photos app. She patted the seat of the stool next to her, and Christine sidled around the table to sit there, where they could look at the pics together.

"I stopped taking pictures after everything went crazy," Amy said, "so we can start at the end and work backwards." She scrolled through pictures until she reached the night in question. "This is the last picture I took."

Christine peered at Amy's phone. It was a shot of Jeff, Joe, and Blaise playing their instruments after they'd started their set. Christine thought back. The band had only played four or five songs before George Booker stopped them, but they hadn't yet started when Scott disappeared, so this shot had to be from minutes after the murder.

The back of Brian's head was clearly visible in the foreground.

"Okay, there he is," Christine said. "But this is after the murder. Do you have any from earlier?"

Amy swiped that picture away to expose a new one. It was very similar to the first and probably taken only seconds earlier. She kept swiping.

"Here's one from before they started playing," Amy said. Brian was in that one as well, sitting in the same chair, but turned around to talk to his friends, so his face was visible.

"What time was that one?" Christine said.

Amy dragged the pic up to expose the time stamp. "Five-fifty-seven."

"Keep going back."

She swiped through several pictures in a row. "Five-fifty-five. Five-forty-nine. Five-forty-nine again. Five-forty-two. Five-forty. Five-thirty-eight."

"That's enough." The shots had all been from different angles, and not all had shown Brian's table, but in all of them that had, he'd been right there in his chair. "He was there the whole time."

Brian Harrison could not have murdered Scott Cornell himself. Unless he'd hired someone else to do the deed, he was cleared.

While flipping through Amy's pictures, Christine had also been paying attention, in the back of her mind, to the parking lot around the deck, in case a random shot of Mark should present itself.

The Mark scenario was one she hated to think about, but one she had to consider. She'd love to find some photographic evidence that exonerated him once and for all. "Do you have any pictures of Mark during that time frame? From inside, maybe?"

"Mark Moody?"

"Yeah."

"Pretty sure I do, actually. It was a couple minutes before I went outside. I took a video of him petting that dog that got kicked. It's really cute." She scrolled backwards through time until she found the picture in question. "Right here."

Christine watched the video, taken from somewhere amongst the tables on the B-side, with a smile. It showed a grinning Mark, bending over at the front door to ruffle Honey's head, with her happy owners watching. The time stamp was five-thirty-six, which did not wholly get Mark off the hook, but it helped. If she could find another one from a few minutes later, she could put it out of her mind for good.

She restarted the video to watch it again. It really was cute.

Amy laughed. "See what I mean?"

"Yeah," Christine said with a chuckle. But as she watched it again, her eye caught a flicker of motion through the window behind Mark, outside the taproom. "Hey," she said, "what's Scott doing outside here?" She could see a man in a Double Groove tie-dye ball cap walking from the parking lot entrance toward the food truck. Most of his body was obscured by the tables and chairs on the deck, but his head, and the hat on it, were not, and the hat was clearly Scott's.

But it couldn't be Scott. If the time stamp was right, this was during the time Scott and Megan had been having a little brouhaha at the bar, or minutes thereafter, a time during which Christine had had her eyes on him. He'd gone straight from the bar back to his table, where he answered a text, then went back toward the brewhouse. There had been no time for him to be outside at all.

"Let me see," Amy said. She took the phone back and watched. "That's not Scott."

"Then why is he wearing Scott's hat?"

"Let me check it out," Jeff said. As he watched the video, he said, "No, that's not Scott. But there's a lot of those hats around. They sold like hotcakes last year."

"Do either of you recognize him?"

"Nope," Amy said.

"I feel like I've seen him here before," Jeff said, "but I've never talked to him. It could be anybody."

Christine took the phone again and watched the video one more time. The man in the tie-dye hat wore a dark sculpted beard, not much longer than a five o'clock shadow. It definitely wasn't Scott, and like Jeff, Christine thought she'd seen him at Double Groove before, but couldn't remember his name. "Is he wearing a jacket?" she said. "He must be nuts. It was like eighty-eight degrees that day."

Both Jeff and Amy looked again, and they confirmed that, from what they could see in glimpses as the man passed between the tables, the man seemed to be wearing long black pants and a maroon zip-up hoodie.

"Huh," Christine said. "Anyway, it's a cute video. You should send it to Mark."

"Already did," Amy said.

"Send it to me, too, if you don't mind."

"Sure, no problem."

Christine waited for the signal from her phone. "Got it," she said. "Thanks for your help, guys. Time for me to go home, it's been a long day."

Outside of the impractical clothing, there was nothing remarkable about the guy in the tie-dye hat out in the parking lot. Except for the fact that Christine didn't remember anyone else wearing a hat similar to Scott's that night. And she was sure she would have noticed. This was a new player on the stage, one no one had known about until now. *Could he be Charlie Hawkins?*

A tiny spark ignited in the back of her mind. Three separate elements—the things she'd just learned from Amy's phone, the revelation of Janis' plagiarism with the subsequent blackmail, and an offhand comment that had come out of the mouth of the author herself yesterday—combined like fuel, air, and fire to finally get Christine's pistons moving.

In her mind's eye, she imagined her new friend Marlin giving her a sly wink.

CHAPTER TWENTY-TWO

STRICTLY SPEAKING, CHRISTINE was already off the clock at Double Groove, but she had two more things to do before she could go home.

First, she went to the brewhouse where she could be alone, haunted Facebook and Instagram for a few minutes, and found further confirmation regarding the suspicion that had been growing in her mind. She saved a few pictures onto her phone. Then she went to Google to get a couple of addresses and put the addresses into the Maps app to see the route between the two and get a travel time. Within ten minutes, she had all the hard supportive data she needed.

More certain than ever that her hunch was on target, she approached Mark.

"This is gonna sound crazy," she said, "but do you think we should have another book signing for Janis O'Riordan? Not the reading and all that. Just to sell and sign books. She didn't get to finish that last weekend."

Mark shrugged. "Not a bad idea. Ask Lisa."

"There's no time. We need to do it as soon as possible, like tomorrow, if we can."

Mark started. "Tomorrow! No way. We need at least a week to get the word out."

"I'll handle that part. All I have to do is call Janis and let her Facebook Fan Club know. The people will show up, believe me."

Mark gave her his *this-is-highly-irregular* look.

"Trust me. This is important. It's not just about the book signing; that's a cover story, to be honest. The real issue is I'm afraid the killer might kill again, if they haven't already, and I have an idea to flush them out before that happens. The longer we wait, the more dangerous it becomes."

Mark stared at her for a good three seconds before saying, "All right then. We'll do it at four-thirty, do you think that'll work?"

"I hope so."

"It better, because it's a Friday night and we have Radio Religion playing at six, so you know how it gets in here."

"I do. Did you talk to Alan and Ronnie about Steven?"

"Yeah. Ronnie's going to run over to Steven's house in a few minutes, see if he's okay."

"Good, it'll save me the trouble. But before he goes, ask him a favor for me? It'd be better if it came from you."

* * *

At last, she could go home. She was dog tired as she left via the back door and got into her vehicle. As soon as the Highlander's Bluetooth connected with her phone, she called Brian Harrison. He understood her intent and was on board with the idea, and said he would ensure Janis was as well. Which was good, Christine mused, because it wouldn't work out at all without her.

Next, she called Shane Ritchie and told him the plan.

"Do you think you can get the word out?" she finished.

"Yes, absolutely. I'll post it as soon as we hang up."

"I was also thinking this would be a chance for you to show your support, since you were unable to make it last time."

"I was thinking the same thing," Shane said. "It's been a long time since we had a chance to hang out, she and I."

"What? I thought you two were great friends?"

"Oh, we are. But I've only met her in person twice. Most of our interaction has been, you know, virtual. Do you know if her husband will be there, by any chance?"

"I assume he will, yes."

"Gotcha. Well, see you tomorrow, then."

"I look forward to meeting you."

She disconnected with Shane as she turned onto her home street. Everything was in place. Now all she had to do was ...

What the hell?

Up ahead in her driveway sat a copper-colored pickup truck.

A copper-colored *1941 Ford* Pickup truck. One exactly like the truck she'd seen only in a picture on her phone, and that had subsequently been sold out from under her.

As she drove closer to the house, she saw her husband and two sons standing out front, talking with a rangy white-haired man in blue jeans and a white wifebeater. They all turned to look at her as she pulled into the driveway and parked behind the truck. Bobby and the boys were smiling. The white-headed guy was not.

She debarked from the Highlander, all senses on high alert. This was the same truck. It had to be. She didn't recognize the surly-looking fellow next to her husband, and could only assume it was the guy who'd bought the truck from Julius. She disliked him already, without even meeting him. But what was he doing here?

"What's going on?" she said. "What's this truck doing here?"

"Happy Thursday," Bobby said.

"Huh?"

"I was gonna save it for Christmas, but you've been some next-level impatient lately. Didn't think I would've got away with it."

Christine stared at him. Stared at the truck. Saw Evan, the younger of her two boys, bouncing up and down on the balls of his feet with suppressed excitement.

"It's yours," Bobby said.

"How ... I mean ... is this the same one we talked about the other night?"

"Yeah."

"But somebody else bought it."

"I did, goofball," Bobby said.

"*You* did?"

"I called him," the older gentleman piped up, "soon's you called me."

It dawned on her. "Julius?" she said.

The older man nodded, scowling.

"I've been dickerin' with him for a month," Bobby said. "Also been stringin' you along with other trucks I knew wouldn't work out, just to keep you off the trail."

"That one in Elkton," Christine said, "you knew about that too?"

"That it was a piece of junk? Yeah. I asked around. Lot of people knew about that guy."

"So the whole trip was staged."

"Yup," Bobby said, smiling.

"You're diabolical."

"And then when you found Julius' truck by yourself," he said, "I like to had a heart attack."

"I didn't find it. Strazz did."

"Yeah, I'm gonna have to have a word with him."

Christine finally allowed herself to smile as the backstory became clear. The hemming and hawing, the lame excuses. She'd been close to spoiling his surprise. She looked at Julius. "Nice acting," she said. "You got me good."

"Still want m'beer," he said. "Price for makin' me lie."

Christine burst out laughing as the reality of the situation began to set in: the truck was hers. "You'll have it," she said. "It's right inside. Afraid I let it get warm, though."

Julius shrugged. "Got an icebox at home."

"Why don't you tell her about the truck, Julius?" Bobby said.

"She's got a GM 327 in her," Julius said.

"I know you would've preferred a traditional flathead," Bobby said.

Christine shrugged. "I'm not complaining."

"'Scuse me," Julius said. "Can I talk?"

Christine stifled a smile and gestured for him to continue.

"Seven hunnert R4 automatic tranny, nine inch three-fitty-five rear. I added disc brakes to the front. Extra crossmembers underneath. Fenders and runnin' boards are all steel." He opened the driver's door. "Tilt column, Dolphin aftermarket gauges. Interior all restored better'n new. Let's look under the hood."

As Julius opened the hood, Christine reflected that he'd just spoken more words than the grand total of all he'd uttered to her yesterday, in two separate conversations.

Christine was more than pleased with the looks of the engine. It was super clean, with chrome intake manifold and valve covers. "Edelbrock carbs," Julius continued, "MSD distributor and coil. I added an A/C condenser." Christine noticed a slight tremble in his hand as he gestured.

"You told me the engine and the interior were a wreck," she said to her husband.

Bobby shrugged. "Again, just tryin' to throw you off the trail."

Christine shook her head with a rueful grin and turned back to Julius. "You do all this work yourself?" she asked.

"Yep. She was a mess when I got 'er. Took eight years."

"I can imagine. Why're you getting rid of her now?"

Julius shrugged. "Need the money. And I can't drive no more after today, really shouldn'ta driven here, neither. Parkinson's."

Christine's hand flew to her mouth. "Sorry to hear that."

Julius shrugged again. "Life. Wanna drive 'er?"

"Love to."

"Good. Need a ride home."

Christine looked at Bobby. He was smiling. "Go ahead," he said. "I'll wait here."

"Can we go?" Kyle asked.

"No," Bobby said. "Let your mom have her drive. There's no seatbelts in the middle, anyway. So, no."

"Don't forget m'beer," Julius said.

* * *

It didn't feel entirely real to her until she was on the way home, after dropping Julius and his beer off at his little rancher in Jarrettsville. The truck was hers.

Hers.

It was mind-boggling.

She thought she detected a slight vibration that could mean new U-joints someday, but nothing to worry about for now, and still a steal at the price Bobby had negotiated. The truck ran sweetly as Christine wound her out on the

East-West Highway, her dual exhaust emitting a pleasant rumble, like a muscle car, but not loud enough to be a nuisance. The old-school bench seat provided little comfort for Christine's back, but her long legs reached the pedals easily at a natural ergonomic angle. The truck steered easily, her brakes felt smooth, acceleration was fantastic, and the transmission shifted smoothly. This truck was a dream come true.

Christine had been so mad at Bobby, while all the time, he'd been plotting to surprise her with this truck. It made her cringe with embarrassment. She felt a gush of emotion, self-reproach mixed with love for her husband, come up from her center and out through her tear ducts.

She'd never overtly expressed anger at him; she just hadn't been very talkative the last couple of nights.

But he knew. He knew she'd wanted to go see the truck two nights ago and he'd shot her down, he knew she'd called Julius yesterday, and he knew she'd been told the truck had been sold to someone else. He'd have to have been pretty obtuse not to have figured out that she'd blamed him. And he was never obtuse.

She had some making up to do.

She arrived at home, parked the truck in the driveway again. They'd already made plans to move the Shelby to Bobby's shop, where he had extra room for storage, so they could keep the truck in the garage at home, but for now, the weather forecast was spectacular, so Christine was comfortable leaving her in the driveway for the time being. Besides, it was her truck, and she wanted it seen.

Inside, she found Bobby on the couch, watching TV as if it were just any day. He looked up as she entered the room, and said, "Oh, hey. Hi."

"Get up, you bastard," she said, smiling.

He rose, returning her smile, and they embraced. "I'm

gonna kill you," she said.

"Right now?"

"Mmmm … no. I think not. Tomorrow, maybe."

CHAPTER TWENTY-THREE

FRIDAY MORNING'S WEATHER forecast predicted no clouds or rain for the next several days, so it would've been a perfect day to take the new truck to Double Groove. But Christine was too nervous about her other plans for the day, and didn't want the distraction of showing the truck off to her coworkers and whomever else saw it or heard about it. So she drove the Highlander to work again.

By the time she got there at five minutes to ten, the temperature had already climbed into the eighties.

She and Kyle spent the morning brewing All Along the Scotchtower, but Christine's mental machinery was whirring, lining up contingency plans for an ever-widening decision tree about whatever might happen later.

Shortly before noon, Steven showed up. Just strolled in as if nothing were amiss.

"Where have you *been*?" Christine said to him.

"At the hospital."

"What hospital? What happened?" Kyle asked.

"What do you mean?" he asked. "I called Lisa Wednesday morning and told her about it."

"Oh, he told *Lisa*," Christine said. Suddenly things made

sense.

"Lisa's been so sick," Kyle said, "she must've forgotten all about it. She never mentioned it to us."

"And Mark probably never even told her we were worried about you," Christine added.

"So, are you okay?" Kyle asked. "Did you get hurt, or …?"

"No, no, it wasn't me," Steven said. "My girlfriend's mom got sick and had to go to Johns Hopkins. We've been down there most of the time."

"Holy crap," Christine said, relieved. "You scared us to death."

"Sorry," Steven said. "Didn't mean to."

"Anyway," Kyle said. "Glad you're not dead."

"You thought I was dead?" Steven said with a laugh.

"It crossed our minds," Christine said.

"So, how's her mom now?" Kyle asked.

"She'll be fine. They put a heart valve from a pig in her; they say it'll last her another thirty years, so that means she'll live to ninety-five."

"How come you never answered our calls?" Christine said.

"Never got any," Steven said. "Couldn't call out from inside that building, either."

"Must be all the metal in the frame," Kyle said.

Steven shrugged. "Beats me. All I know is, we didn't have any cell reception at all in there."

"Well, anyway," Christine said, "good to have you back." She kept her huge sigh of relief figurative, but it took an effort. She'd already stopped wondering if Steven had himself been the killer, but she still had to worry about whether he'd become the second victim … until now. Talk about a load off her mind.

The taproom opened at noon. Christine was as mentally

prepared for today's little drama as she could be, but there was no reason to take on the physical aspects of it by herself when she had perfectly good muscle at her disposal. She called Michael and asked him to come back to the brewhouse, and she had a brief discussion with Michael and Kyle, both of whom assured her they were comfortable with their parts.

Michael returned to the taproom, and Christine followed to help him and Steven, while Kyle stayed in the brewhouse. The usual cast of bar-sitters, the sheriff and Ronnie Gaines among them, showed up, and the early afternoon went smoothly.

Around three o'clock, Christine first started to notice the arrival of some new faces, and there were more women than would be ordinarily expected, some of them in pairs or trios. Janis O'Riordan fans. It looked like Shane had done a good job of getting the word out.

Mark appeared, along with a recovered but abjectly apologetic Lisa. "Sorry, I haven't gotten to that database we talked about yet," she said to Christine.

"That's okay," Christine said. "We might not need it at all after today. What you *should* be sorry about is not telling us about Steven calling out."

Lisa's hand flew to her mouth. "Oh my God, I'm so sorry."

Michael, Steven, and Christine all laughed. "No harm, no foul," Michael said. "We figured it out."

"Yeah, about an hour ago," Christine said, rolling her eyes.

At four o'clock, Janis and Brian showed up, and started setting up their table in the corner again. No Tina Cornell, which wasn't a surprise. She was probably getting fresh lip filler for her husband's funeral. No matter. Tina was not on Christine's short list.

Regis and Angela Burke came next, and a few minutes later, John and Sue Harris, Rick and Stella Rineer, Strazz, and Randy Frey, along with a diverse assortment of regulars and strangers. Meanwhile, Radio Religion had arrived and begun setting up their equipment on the deck for the night's show, and two of the three Willig Boys, with wives in tow, had pulled in as spectators, not as performers this time.

By four-thirty, the place was packed again. It almost reminded Christine of last Saturday, and this was on one day's notice, without Lisa's help in advertising and push notifications. Quite a testimonial to Shane's power as the administrator of a Facebook page for mystery nerds.

Christine eyes swept over the room. *Not yet.* For a few more minutes, she kept an eye on the doors, watching as patrons filed in, and when she judged the time was right, she nodded to Mark.

The entire cast was back on the hay wagon. Time to roll.

Mark, on his cue, went to the lectern once again, and gave a speech similar to the one he'd given six days earlier. Janis followed him with a few words before sitting down behind her table, as a line of O'Riordan groupies began to form in front of it.

Christine made her move.

She slipped into the brewhouse and found Kyle's phone on the table, right where she'd expected it to be. She stood at the bottom of the stairs leading to the loft, and using Kyle's phone, sent a text.

Christine (as Kyle): I know what you did

Less than a minute later, the reply came.

Unknown number: Who is this

Christine (as Kyle): Come to brewhouse and find out. We can make an arrangement

Moments later, as Christine stared at Kyle's phone waiting for a response, a new text came in.

Michael: Here he comes

Then Christine heard the brewhouse door open, and in strode the man with the sculpted beard. He glanced around, found Christine, and faced her with his mouth open. "What is this?" he said. "Who are you?"

"Hello, Shane," Christine said. "I was hoping you could make it. I'm Christine. We spoke on the phone? And I think you know what this is."

CHAPTER TWENTY-FOUR

"IF I KNEW what this was," Shane said. "I wouldn't be asking you." He was a slight guy with a beaked nose, but appeared by his attitude to find himself imposing.

"How would you describe your relationship with Janis?"

Shane shook his head. "What? What do you mean? I told you, we're friends. That's what you want to talk about?"

"Close friends?"

"Yeah, I suppose. Not sure what you're getting at here."

"In fact," Christine said, "you're attracted to her, aren't you?"

Shane hesitated before answering. "Are you nuts? She's got twenty years on me."

She hadn't been sure up until now, but that tiny delay, half a second if that, had told Christine all she needed to know: Shane was smitten with Janis. He'd created a fan page devoted to her, after all. It didn't take much of a logical leap to go from *superfan* to *obsessed weirdo*. "Good answer, Shane," she said. "But I'm not buying it."

"I might be a bit protective of her," he said, "I admit. But those other guys, her husbands ... they disrespected her. They weren't worthy."

"And you are?"

"I never said that! Don't put words in my mouth. You know what I think? I think you're just jealous. *You* want me."

Christine blinked. *That* was a response she hadn't seen coming. "I assure you," she said, "that's not the case."

"Then why are you all up in my face about Janis?"

"Because I think you care so much for her that, when you found out Scott Cornell was going to expose her plagiarism, you took it upon yourself to remove him from the equation, and the fact that he was her first husband, well … maybe that was just the icing."

Shane scoffed. "Now I *know* you're crazy. I explained to you before that I was at my sister's wedding that day. There's plenty of photographic proof, if you don't believe me."

And there it was. It wasn't anything Shane said … it was what he *didn't* say that cemented it for Christine. He *didn't* profess ignorance about Janis' plagiarism, or outrage over the accusation. That meant he'd already known. Janis had confided in him at some point, and now Christine knew what Janis had been trying to hide when Shane's name had come up over coffee. Maybe the two of them really did have a fling going on. Christine didn't know and it didn't matter.

"Yeah, about that proof," she said. "I checked out your sister's wedding on Facebook. It was very beautiful, by the way. And you're right, you're in a lot of pictures, both at the wedding at Mount Zion, and at the reception at Jarrettsville Fire Hall."

"So why are we talking about this then?"

"Because," she said, "the wedding was at four-thirty, and the reception was at six. Let's say the ceremony lasted a half hour."

"Seems about right. So what?"

"So, let's say you and the rest of the wedding party hung around fifteen or twenty minutes afterward for pictures before leaving for the reception."

Shane shrugged. "Maybe. I didn't pay much attention."

"Let's say it was fifteen. That would put you leaving Mount Zion at five-fifteen. It's a twenty-three-minute trip from the church to the fire hall, and the route passes within a few hundred feet of where we're standing right now. It would have cost you virtually nothing, timewise, to detour through here on the way. And that would have put you here ... hmm, let's see ... right about the time of the murder."

"That's ridiculous. In my tux? I would've stuck out like a sore thumb."

Christine stuck a finger in the air. "Exactly. That's why you wore a hoodie over your tux and put on a tie-dye Double Groove cap, to disguise the fact that you were dressed for a wedding. And maybe you thought it might hide you from the cameras, as well. I have you on video. Look, I'll show you."

Christine pulled out her phone and accessed Amy's video of Mark petting Honey, with the mystery man walking across the parking lot in the background, and disappearing behind the food truck. She started the video, and angled the phone toward Shane. "Don't watch Mark and the dog," she said. "Watch out the window."

Shane leaned forward to take in the video. "That could be anybody," he said.

"Anybody with a sculpted beard like the one you're rocking right now."

"Everybody has these now."

"I'll give you that," Christine said with a nod. "And at

first, I had no idea who it was, but then I remembered seeing your picture on your fanpage for Janis. So I went back to it and checked, and you can't miss the facial resemblance. It's you. And if that's not enough, look at the color of the hoodie. Maroon, right?"

"Yeah, so?"

"Now," she said, swiping to another picture, "look at this shot I got from the reception. If I zoom in close on you, can you see the little pills of lint all over your tux? Here, on your left shoulder, and here, on your breast pocket? And here, and here?"

"So?"

"Maroon lint. From the fleece lining of that hoodie. If I go back a few pics to the ones from the church," she said, swiping again, then turning the phone back to Shane, "you can see the lint's not there yet. Because that was before you came to Double Groove and pulled that hoodie over your tux."

Shane's eyes darted around the room. "Doesn't prove anything."

"No, it doesn't, but it's enough for me to make up a story. Wanna hear my story?"

"Not really."

"I think you left that wedding and came here. I think you put on that hoodie and that ball cap, and you parked out on Robin Circle and walked around the building and went in the back door."

Shane gave his head a little shake of denial at the end of each accusation.

"I think you hid in the brewhouse," Christine continued, "and you texted Scott Cornell to get him to come back here and meet you, sort of the way I just did to you. Then you put on a pair of gloves out of that box right there on the desk, and you plucked that bulldog pipe off its hook on the wall, and you stood right over there next to the canning machine … and waited."

"Seriously, what is wrong with you? I did no such thing."

"When Scott came through the door and walked past you, you whanged him on the back of the neck, and he fell onto the ledge, where he broke his nose and bled all over the floor."

Shane began shaking his head violently. "Not true. None of this is true."

"You knelt beside him because you wanted to find his phone and delete the text you'd sent to him, but you didn't have time with the body lying there in plain view from the bathrooms, so you just took his phone and dropped it in your pocket. But when you bent over him, your hat fell off, and the bill of it fell into the blood on the floor, and it got some on it."

"You're out of your mind."

"You said that before, yeah. I have more pictures I want to show you, so you'll know I'm not out of my mind. First there's this one. It shows you with your tie-dye hat on. It was taken at Double Groove earlier this year, on June thirteenth."

"Wow. You got me there."

"Here's another one. This shows Scott Cornell wearing *his* tie-dye hat. It was also taken at Double Groove, on September fourth of last year."

"Seriously," he said with a nervous laugh, "what's the big deal? We both got the same hat. A lot of people did."

"You might think they're the same hat, and no one would blame you. But every tie-dye is different, and sometimes you have to look closely to tell the difference. Both your hat and Scott's hat were done in blue and green dye. But if you really look, you can see they're not the same. See here, on Scott's hat, where a green swirl comes down to the right of the DG logo?"

Shane nodded.

"And on the other side of the logo is a blue swirl. Now look at this closeup of *your* hat. The stripe to the right of the logo is blue, and the one on the *left* is green. They're reversed, and shaped a little differently as well. Not enough that anyone would notice, unless they looked closely, but the difference is clear once you do. So, here's the rest of my story: You dragged Scott's body over here next to the stairs, and then you bent down to pick up your hat, and you saw it had blood on it. You probably had a little moment of panic, but then you noticed that Scott's hat was also on the floor, and *miracle of miracles*, it was also a Double Groove tie-dye hat in blue and green *just like yours*. Only his didn't have any blood on it, because it flew off his head when you hit him, before his face hit the floor and made him bleed. So you dropped *your* hat back on the floor, and you put *Scott's* hat on your head, and you walked out the back door again, with the pipe and Scott's cellphone and Scott's hat. You broke into the back door of Not Just Vacs, stashed the pipe, ran back around the building to your car, pulled the SIM card from Scott's phone, and drove to your sister's reception. You were probably a few minutes late, but I doubt anyone noticed."

"That whole story is absurd," he said.

"Really? What would you say if I told you the pattern of the hat that's in police custody right now, the one with blood on it, matches the one on your head in this old picture?"

Shane took a moment to answer. "That's not possible. You're lying. I'm innocent."

Christine shook her head with a little smile. "The ironic thing is, if you'd just taken your hat with you and thrown it away somewhere, you might've gotten away with it. But you panicked, and you made a mistake."

"These are all lies, and I hope you haven't told anyone else about your little theory. My reputation is very important to me, and if even a hint of this gets out, it won't matter that I'm innocent. They'll roast me alive."

"Oh, your reputation is safe for now. This is between you and me."

"Good."

"But I've got an open mind. You keep telling me I'm wrong, so tell me how I'm wrong. If you didn't drop your hat on the floor there yourself, then tell me how it got there, with Scott's blood on it. I'm all ears."

Christine's Plan A had been to somehow trick or goad Shane into making a confession, but so far, that hadn't worked out. He continued to stick to his guns, and that meant it might be time to go to Plan B.

Shane's eyes moved around the room. They covered the walls, the doors, the tables, the floor, the ferm tanks.

"Looking for another way out?" Christine asked him. "The back door's locked. Or maybe you're looking for a weapon, but you won't find one, Shane. We hid everything big enough to clobber somebody with. Oh, wait, I forgot." She picked something up off the table next to her. "Here's a rubber band. Would you like it? You could shoot me with it, maybe."

Shane's lips twisted as a snarl escaped from his throat. "I didn't want to have to do this," he said, and he charged Christine with a roar, hands up and aiming for her throat. He slammed into her, knocking her backward against the stair railing, and then down to the floor, where his weight pinned her. The breath whooshed out of her lungs as she felt ribs pop, and his hands locked around her neck.

"Damn you," he said into her face as he increased the pressure, "Why couldn't you have just butted out? Now look what you've made me do!"

This had gone all wrong. Yes, this was Plan B, but Christine hadn't anticipated the sheer ferocity of his attack, and in her pain and shock, she had failed to draw another breath before his thumbs closed her windpipe. She was terrified to find that she was already out of air. In her panic, she did all the wrong things. She made a futile and oxygen-wasting attempt to push him off her bodily. When that didn't work, she launched a feeble and poorly-aimed punch that hit him in the left ear, to no effect. She knew she was close to blacking out, and once that happened, she would die.

She needn't have worried. Shane's weight disappeared and his hands slipped from her neck as Kyle, who had emerged from his hiding place behind a fern tank, pulled him off of her. Michael then burst into the room and added his strength, lifting Shane into the air and tossing him aside to land in a crumpled, groaning, undignified heap.

Christine took a great gasp of blessed air as she sat up.

"Get your hands behind your head!" Ronnie Gaines yelled as he thundered down the stairs from the loft, service weapon trained on Shane. Sheriff Alan Curtis came pounding in his wake. "You're under arrest!"

CHAPTER TWENTY-FIVE

CHRISTINE CROUCHED BEHIND the bar, nerves on edge, trying to remain as quiet as possible. On either side of her cowered Lisa and Kyle, and beside them, Mark, Michael, and Steven, all of whom remained silent as well.

In the silence, the sound of the A-side door opening may as well have been a gunshot. Christine heard footsteps enter the room.

"What the hell is this?" came a voice.

* * *

Three hours earlier, Christine had been drinking coffee in her back yard and enjoying the birth of another beautiful summer day. It was the day after Shane Ritchie's arrest, and Christine felt a sense of peace and relaxation she hadn't known since the day before Scott Cornell died. Shane was in jail. Charges against Megan had been dropped, and she was coming back to work. Christine had a wonderful husband and two awesome kids in the house behind her, and the world's sweetest pickup truck in her garage. And the weather was perfect.

Her ribs were sore as hell and it hurt to laugh, but given the circumstances, it was a small price to pay.

In addition to her ribs, another small disappointment marred the perfection of this day: that one of Christine's favorite authors had turned out to be a cheater, a recycler of old TV plots.

Christine also knew that once the news of Janis' plagiarism got out, the message boards would be all over it, and Christine suspected that more of Janis O'Riordan's novels would soon prove to be stolen, just as *Death of the Blues* had been.

Still, Christine had no intention of letting anything, ribs or cheaters, spoil this day.

She finished her coffee, said goodbye to her men, and backed the pickup out of her garage. Today, the new truck would make her debut at Double Groove. She'd already texted Rick Rineer and learned that he would also be bringing his '67 Chevelle, and Ed Raither would be bringing his '77 'Vette as well, creating the seed for what could turn into an impromptu car show in the brewery's parking lot.

She was looking forward to this evening. She had plans to meet Marlin at a local retailer for outdoorsmen, where he would help her pick out her own fly rod. Then she could give him his loaner back, and she could tell him how on-target his advice had been. She felt like he deserved at least some of the credit for what she'd been able to accomplish.

But first, she had a shift at Double Groove to get out of the way. It would be Megan's first day back, and Christine couldn't wait to hug her friend. Gingerly.

When she arrived, Mark and Lisa greeted her outside.

"Wow," Mark said as they made a circuit around Christine's truck. "It really is a beauty."

"Thanks," Christine said. She felt tears building. Warring

emotions—among them, relief that Mark hadn't proven to be guilty of anything, shame from having kept him in suspicion in the back of her mind for so long, and good old-fashioned unadulterated joy—drove her to step forward and embrace her boss.

"Congratulations," Lisa said, smiling behind her husband. "You deserve this."

Christine, separating from Mark, nodded and hugged Lisa in turn.

After an appropriate time spent oohing and ahhing, Mark said, "Come on inside. Wanna show you something."

When they stepped inside the A-side door, the first thing Christine saw was a huge banner suspended over the bar, reading "WELCOME BACK MEGAN" in bold purple letters. Purple streamers and whirligigs hung from all the light fixtures. The entire brewery had been transformed into an expression of Megan's favorite color.

"Hey, Christine," a grinning Steven said from behind the bar. "Welcome to the party."

"I have one more surprise," Mark said. "Today we're gonna announce a new beer in Megan's honor. It's that raspberry ale we talked about last month, and it'll be called Purple Reign."

"Okay," Christine said, "now we're getting over the top with the purple."

"That's what I said," Steven said, "but wait'll you hear the rest. It's worth it."

Mark shrugged, smiling. "I was gonna do it anyway, but I had it planned for football season. I just bumped the schedule up a little. And one last thing: for one day only, the day it's released, all sales of Purple Reign will go to a fund to help defray Megan's legal bill."

"We're gonna have a big Sunday festival that day," Lisa added. "The Willig Boys were already on the schedule, and we're talking to some other bands to help out."

Christine shook her head. "You guys are amazing."

Mark and Christine spent the morning making and boiling the wort for the new raspberry ale and transferring it to a fermentation tank, where it would spend a couple of weeks before being canned.

Fifteen minutes before Megan was due to arrive, the entire staff, including Michael and Kyle, who weren't even on the schedule today, assembled behind the bar. They watched until they saw Megan's car pull in and park, then they all crouched down.

Megan came in, and Christine heard her say, "What the hell is this?"

Collectively, the staff of Double Groove Brewing sprang to their feet as they yelled, "Surprise!"

Megan's hands flew to her face as she screamed. "Holy smokes," she said. "You guys scared the crap out of me."

Christine and the others filed out from behind the bar to join Megan in the taproom for a group hug. Abundant smiles and laughter were punctuated with frequent high fives, amid a sprinkling of tears.

"Welcome back," Lisa said.

"Oh my God, I love you guys so much," Megan said. "But none of this could've happened without you, Christine."

"Eh," Christine said with a shrug. "This isn't about me. This is your day."

"No," Mark said. "she's right. We have you to thank for this. Let's hear it for Christine!"

* * *

The taproom opened at noon, and although the banner and the whirligigs remained, the theme of the party was soon forgotten as the afternoon gradually morphed into a normal Saturday at Double Groove. A cast of regulars flowed in, starting with Ronnie and the Sheriff, and followed by the Harrises, the Rineers, the Willigs, Strazz, and the Burkes. In due time Randy Frey and Jerry McKernan arrived, along with Mike and Michele DiPietro, Mark and Carmella Taylor, and Jim Geckle, Double Groove's go-to artist, who had rendered all their beer can labels and posters, and with him came his wife, Lori. Brian Harrison even put in a solo appearance, sans spouse.

At one point, Christine noticed a familiar face sitting with Ronnie and the Sheriff. "You gotta be kidding me," she muttered.

She moved over to the end of the bar where they sat. "Detective Kingery," she said, "I barely recognized you in a t-shirt."

Kingery smiled and extended his hand to her. "Call me Bruce," he said. "I came to offer my apologies to Ms. Gravell and congratulations to you."

Christine shrugged. "I just got lucky. What would you like, Bruce?"

"I'll take a Back in Black Cherry, please, and that was more than luck, but we'll leave it at that. Do you think Megan will accept my apology?"

"She's a tough one, but I think she'll respect the fact that you had nerve enough to show up here on her first day back. All I can say is, good luck."

"You!" Megan said from behind Christine. Christine turned to see Megan march across to the B-side and come face to face with Kingery, her eyebrows lowered and a frown on her lips.

"Ms. Gravell," Kingery began.

"I know you were just doing your job," she said. "I know you were following the evidence."

Kingery nodded.

Megan turned tail and walked away.

"That," Christine said, "was about the best you could've hoped for. Give her time, she'll be fine."

"She won't spit in my beer or anything, will she?" Kingery said.

"She would never. And besides, I'm getting your beer. As soon as you give me your card."

The taps flowed freely as both the taproom and the deck began to fill up, while Russ May and Johnny Benson started setting up for their Celtic grunge punk metal show under the canopy. Mark, Lisa, Christine, and Steven manned the taps, tables, rags, and mops, while Kyle and Michael joined the merrymakers. Christine's truck and the other classic cars offered a pleasant diversion for everyone, especially the gearheads in the crowd. People came and people went, with the core group remaining steady, and it was a good thing all of them had either brought designated drivers or lived within walking distance.

Russ and Johnny played everything from Johnny Cash to Black Sabbath along with their usual assortment of Irish tunes, working the crowd up to a thirsty frenzy. For their last song, Johnny climbed atop the bar with his violin to play his lightning-fast version of "John Ryan's Polka," while Russ roamed among the tables, ferociously strumming rhythm guitar like a crazed Christy Moore, and the delighted crowd clapped along. Christine, taking it all in, smiled with a sense of comfort that was well-earned and a long time coming.

It was another typical day at Double Groove Brewing.

THE END

ACKNOWLEDGEMENTS

Incalculable thanks to the owners of Double Groove Brewing, Mark Moody, Lisa Moody, and Kyle Waters, for not only giving me permission to use their business as the setting for a fictional murder, but also for encouraging me—rather insistently, in fact—to undertake this project. Thanks are due to them also for the production of some mighty fine beer, which rescued the year 2020 from the cesspool of Hell and made it tolerable, and has continued to be a force for good in the lives of many, including mine, ever since.

Thanks also to the other staff members at Double Groove: Megan Gravell, Steven Kutcher, Michael Reisinger, and of course Christine Buckley, who, now that I think of it, actually owes me one for not only making her a hero, but also for subtracting ten years from her real age. *SHHH!* Did I say that out loud?

The same applies to Christine's husband Bobby Buckley, and her two sons, Evan and Kyle, all of whom I made younger for my own mysterious and probably dastardly reasons, which will become clear in any purely hypothetical (at this point) sequels.

Thanks to the owner of Not Just Vacs, Mike Parker, for kindly giving me permission to use the name of his business. Thanks as well to all three Willig Boys, Jeff Willig, Blaise Willig, and Joe Wilson, for allowing me to use them fictitiously, and to Craig and Donna Willig, former co-owners of Double Groove, for the same largesse. Thanks to Radio Religion, Second Wind, Russ May, and Johnny Benson for allowing me to use their personal and band names.

Thanks to Jim Geckle, who not only provides the artwork and design for all of Double Groove's beer cans and posters, but also the stunning covers for all of my novels to date, including this one. And let's not forget Jim's amazingly talented (and tolerant) wife Lori, who not only allowed me to use her name, but willingly undertakes the Herculean task of keeping Jim on the straight and narrow.

Thanks are also due to Double Groove homies Regis and Angela Burke, Mike and Michele DiPietro, John and Sue Harris, Phyllis Hemmes, Mike Karavas, Rick and Stella Rineer, Mike Strazzire, and Amy Willig for allowing me to write them into this novel without any real idea of the extent to which I might distort them into something they're not. (Or even kill them!) I hope I haven't offended.

Finally, thanks to accomplished author Robert Broomall and the members of the Bel Air Creative Writing Association: Alan Amrhine, Luke Bullis, Sarah Burgess, Terry Emery, Tom Ewald, Ken Godfrey, Matt Hasek, Keith Hoskins, Lisa Janele, Mark Matthews, Kim Monaco, and Eileen Szychowski, for their valuable input and admirable restraint.

Finally—and I know I said finally before, but this is for real—a big overflowing bucket of gratitude to my wonderful wife Carmella, who tolerates my taciturnity and distractedness while I'm writing a novel, all in the name of promoting the arts. I love you, Carmella, and I owe you big time. Put it on my tab, okay?

A NOTE FROM THE AUTHOR

If you've already been to Double Groove Brewing, then you know about the beer. I don't have to tell you anything. But if you haven't been, put it on your list. I promise you, you won't be disappointed, and you just might find me sitting at the bar.

Don't go there hoping to find a tie-dye hat, though. They don't exist. I made that shit up.

I hope you enjoyed this book. If I've done anything to improve your day, and you'd like to return the favor, the best thing you can do for me is to leave a review on Amazon. If you're uncomfortable with that, just tell a friend about this book. Word of mouth is everything.

See you at the Groove.

ABOUT THE AUTHOR

Mark Lee Taylor, an acknowledged Deadhead, Star Wars geek, and baseball fan, is the author of the novels *A Pebble Tossed* and *Foul Territory* and the novella *Manaia*. He lives, with his wife Carmella, within spitting distance of Double Groove Brewing, which is either a boon or a curse, depending on how you look at it.

To learn more about Mark Lee Taylor and his writings, visit his website at www.markleetaylorauthor.com.

Made in the USA
Middletown, DE
03 September 2024

60244008R00126